Full Coverage:
An Action Comedy

Tom Reeve

Dedicated to my parents,
who always encourage me to act out on my silly ideas.

Special Thanks to Chris, Christine, Cory, Crystal, Jeff, Joe, John, Julie, Liz, Nan, Olivia, Pat, Reena and Sara, for helping with this book!

CHAPTER ONE

Kyle Soliano pounded on the foot-thick steel door. The midday sun had heated the metal surface to a scorching degree, and his fist had already turned pink from a first-degree burn. Sweat rolled from his spiky hair down his impeccably tanned skin and circled his eyes. He had decided to try bright green this time. Kyle turned to face the breeze as he waited for a response from the Hideki Yakuza clan compound.

The cool air lifted much of the sweat off his face and even more from the sweat wicking shirt beneath the plating of his body armor. The doorway stood inside the ten foot tall white adobe wall that lined the perimeter of the compound. A long driveway curved behind him, leading to a helicopter pad and a boat dock on the beach below. It had been a while since Kyle had taken a job on a private island. On the downside, it meant it took longer to get in and out. On the upside, it meant he didn't have to worry about any nosy neighbors witnessing his actions.

The window on the door slid open. Two suspicious eyes

scanned up and down the body of the sweaty, six-foot-five Samoan, clad head to toe in body armor with a large, blue duffle bag strapped to his back.

"Who are you?" The man behind the door asked.

"Is Boss Lito Hideki there?" Kyle asked in return. "I'd like to have a few words with him if I could."

"There isn't anybody here by that name." The man replied sternly. Two automated minigun turrets popped up from underneath flowerpots on each side of the driveway. The turrets spun around and pointed at Kyle. The hibiscus flowers on top of them bobbed lightly in the breeze. "Go now, or there will be trouble."

"Oh, no, I wouldn't want that. Sorry, my mistake. Bye then." Kyle waved to the man and turned away from the door.

The window on the door scraped shut. Kyle walked away from the door. After a few steps the turrets sank back into the ground until only bright orange flowers were visible.

Kyle took a few more steps and then checked over his shoulder. The window was completely shut. He pulled off his duffle bag and gently laid it down on the red bricked path. He pulled out a reinforced helmet and put it on. A thick layer of bulletproof plastic shielded his face while multiple layers of ceramic, Kevlar and non-Newtonian fluid encased the rest of his head. He wore similar multi-layered armor over the rest of his body.

Next, Kyle pulled out a hulking 20mm machine gun. A bucket sized ammunition drum filled to the brim with explosive tipped rounds hung from the bottom of it. Kyle's burly fingers melded into the cold metal of the custom printed handles. Filed down edges where the gun had been severed from the turret of a small armored vehicle rubbed against the inside of his arms.

He zippered up the duffle bag and tossed it back over his shoulder. The remaining contents shifted to the bottom of the bag.

Kyle heard the whirring mechanical sound of the turrets coming back up out of the ground. Someone must have noticed the giant autocannon he was now holding. With two thunderous bursts of his gun the turrets exploded apart. Burning gears and freshly scrapped metal joined the hibiscus flowers in their new soil.

Three more chest thumping shots blew the metal door off its hinges. The heavy steel door collapsed on to the guard behind it. Kyle stomped down on the fallen door as he entered the compound. Bits of brain squished out from underneath the scorched metal and began to sizzle on the hot stone path.

Alarms rang from all directions. There were only seven buildings in the compound, fewer than Kyle had expected. He pulled out a C4 explosive charge from his duffle bag and tossed it into the guard shack behind him. The explosion rocked the compound. Tiles in the path trembled from the blast. Adobe dust from the pulverized building showered over Kyle.

Yakuza thugs streamed out from the buildings on both sides of the large mansion at the end of the roundabout driveway. A flood of black suits armed with submachine guns and machetes flowed into the gaps between the buildings and barreled towards him.

He squeezed the trigger on his machine gun and the thumping recoil from each shot shook the dust off his body. Explosive rounds tore apart the bodies of the guards at the head of the charge. Rib cages, arms and various pieces of flesh littered the manicured lawn and the walking paths that ran through it. The guards who survived the initial barrage scrambled to take cover behind buildings and opened fire. Shockwaves rippled out over Kyle's chest like drops of water in a lake as the non-Newtonian fluid layer of his body armor dispersed the energy from their bullets, while all Kyle felt was a light smacking on his chest. He slowly walked towards the guards, his machine gun blasting away with each step, blowing chunks out of the buildings they hid behind and then blowing chunks out of them.

A group of three guards darted out from the doorway next to Kyle with their machetes raised. The leader jammed his blade between the armor plates on Kyle's thigh. The edge of the knife dug into his quadriceps until it got stuck in the super dense blood and enhanced muscles under Kyle's plasticized skin. Kyle looked over his shoulder and saw the guard tugging on his machete, trying to free it from Kyle's leg. He lifted his leg and drove it into the guard's chest. Through his boot Kyle could feel a rib give, but the roar of his machine gun drowned out the sound of the snapping bone. The guard flew backwards and knocked over the others who had followed him out as he fell back through the doorway.

Kyle pulled out another C4 charge out and tossed it on top of the pile of guards. As he walked away the earth shook from the explosion. Pieces of ceramic clinked against the brick walkway as pieces of the roof rained down around him.

The shockwave reverberated through the machete stuck in his leg. Kyle kicked with his leg but the machete stubbornly refused to let go. No big deal, he could still move freely and he would have time to pull it out later.

A normal person would have had their eardrums blown out and gone deaf from all the explosions and gunfire by this point, but Kyle's eardrums had been printed with an extra reinforcing layer of plastic. To counter the rejection of plastic from his body, Kyle took plasticizing supplement pills to keep his eardrums strong and his skin shiny and knife resistant.

Two guards got on top of the mansion at the center of the compound and started shooting at Kyle. A few quick thumps from his machine gun tore the legs off one and the chest off the other. Chunks of guards fell down to the ground in front of the mansion as Kyle continued walking towards it.

A large caliber bullet slammed into his head and knocked it sideways. His helmet spun around and obscured his vision. He twisted his helmet back and then looked to see where it had come from. A sniper was standing on top of one of the guard towers taking aim at Kyle.

Kyle took his finger off the trigger and grabbed a C4

charge. With his other hand he pulled out his phone and started recording a video with the camera printed into his eye. Each of Kyle's eyes contained a tiny display that projected information directly on to his retina in addition to a built in camera that could capture anything he could see.

He started the five second timer on the charge and held it for two seconds before flinging it at the tower. The explosive detonated just in front of the sniper. The blast blew off the top part of the guard tower and sent the flaming body of the sniper hurtling to the ground behind it.

Kyle smiled as he stopped the recoding. This would be an excellent video for his portfolio. He tapped the upload button on his phone and continued to make his way towards the mansion.

The remaining guards had taken cover behind the armored limousine that was parked in front of two very brightly colored Lamborghinis at the end of the roundabout just in front of the mansion. Kyle strolled over to them. Gunfire glanced off his clothes and helmet and knocked the machete out of his thigh.

He tossed a C4 charge at the armored limousine. The bomb skidded along the searing asphalt and underneath the limo. The explosion lifted the limo up and flung it into guards hiding behind it, crushing them between the flaming limo and the two Lamborghinis.

More henchmen streamed out from the sides of the main complex. Kyle smiled as he held the trigger down and obliterated the first group of guards coming at him. The deafening roar of machine gun fire and explosions echoed throughout the courtyard.

Kyle kept the trigger down as he turned to annihilate a group of guards on the other side of the mansion. Explosive rounds punched holes across the face of the building as he pivoted around. He glanced at the clock that floated in his field of vision as part of his eyes-only display. Things were going well and he was ahead of schedule. He would definitely get back in time to catch the baseball game.

Suddenly, a black streak rushed down through Kyle's vision and cut into the barrel of his machine gun.

The next round slammed into the obstruction and the explosive tip detonated inside the gun. The explosion tore the barrel apart and knocked Kyle backwards on to the ground. Pieces of searing hot shrapnel penetrated through his clothing and cut into his chest and legs.

Kyle blinked his eyes but all he could see was the glare from the sun shining down into his face. He cursed himself for forgetting to pack the sun visor for his helmet. He shook his head and looked around. A ninja dressed in black with metallic gold eyes stood over him holding a smoldering black machete.

The Latin Yakuza still used katanas for formal occasions like birthday parties and executions, but they had adopted the local machete for their day to day dismemberment needs.

With both arms Kyle pushed off and tried to leap to his feet, but the ninja slammed his foot down into Kyle's chest and shoved him back to the ground. This ninja was strong; his body must have been enhanced like Kyle's.

The ninja thrust the smoking end of his machete at Kyle's face and drove it through the bulletproof plastic facemask on Kyle's helmet. The machete got stuck just before it could reach his eye.

The ninja yanked Kyle's helmet off and tossed it aside.

Kyle tried to roll away. The ninja brought down a second machete and Kyle blocked it with his forearm. The edge of the machete cut into a gap in his armor plating. Enhanced muscles in the ninja's body drove it deep into Kyle's arm, but it got stuck when it jammed into one of Kyle's silicate infused bones.

"Ha! What are you going to do now?" Kyle taunted the ninja as he tugged on his machete, trying to get it out of his arm.

The ninja punched Kyle in the face. The force of the impact drove Kyle's head backwards into the tiled path he was lying on. Adobe bricks cracked from the impact underneath his head.

"That all you got?" Kyle yelled at the bright spot in his vision.

Kyle saw the ninja's gloved fist come down a second time and then nothing but black.

CHAPTER TWO

Ice cold water splashed against Kyle's face and jolted him awake. An old man holding a bucket stood in front of him with a smile and a scar on his face. Cold iron shackles that chained him to the floor rubbed against his arms. Kyle was on his knees on the bare concrete floor. Cold water ran down his face and over the bare skin of his arms and chest. His armored plated shirt hung off the side of a steel table next to the old man. One of the arms had been cut off of it. Blood dripped from the shirt on to the concrete.

The clock in his eyes-only display showed that two hours had passed. He had missed the start of the game!

The ninja walked next to him and tugged on the handle of his machete as he struggled to dislodge it from Kyle's arm. The cut was deep, but the bone had held. The ninja put his foot against Kyle's shoulder and yanked the machete free. Syrupy blood oozed from the gash and seeped down his arm.

Like many divers and professional soldiers of fortune, Kyle took pills that increased the density of his blood and supersaturated it with oxygen. These pills worked in conjunction with other pills containing artificial enzymes that converted fat to muscle, boosting the strength of his heart and muscles while also allowing Kyle to strength train by eating cheeseburgers.

Boss Lito Hideki entered through the only opening in the chamber, a steel door on the far side of the room from Kyle. Two bodyguards wearing sunglasses followed him in carrying briefcases in one hand and submachine guns in the other. The walls of the rest of the cell were bare aside from the light in the ceiling and the drain in the floor in front of him.

The old man and the ninja bowed to their boss as he entered.

"Diego, I see you have caught me a present." Boss Hideki said as he nodded back to them.

"Thank you boss." Diego said as he bowed again. "He is an assassin. An enhanced one."

"Marcelo, what have you found?" Hideki turned an inquisitive gaze towards Kyle. Kyle winked back.

"Nothing yet boss. We waited until you arrived to wake him."

"Very good." One of the bodyguards placed a stool a few feet from Kyle and the second one wiped it off with his handkerchief. Hideki sat down and examined Kyle more closely. The two bodyguards flanked him, submachine guns and briefcases at the ready. "Who are you working for assassin?"

"I'm afraid that if you are thinking about making a

counteroffer, then you will have to go through the proper channels instead. These on the spot things are really frowned upon in the industry." Kyle replied.

This was true. Accepting counteroffers generally resulted in poor reviews and the former client putting a fresh hit out on you.

Hideki winked to Diego. The ninja nodded, then calmly walked over to Kyle and grabbed his head. Diego plunged his thumb and first two fingertips into Kyle's right eye socket, working them behind the slippery orb inside. With a quick yank, he plucked out the eye and snapped the optic nerve connected to it. He tossed the eye to the floor, stepped on it and walked back to the side of Boss Hideki.

"Dammit! I just got that replaced!" Kyle yelled at them.

With one eye missing, the clock and heading indicator in his eyes-only display became distorted. If he couldn't change the settings soon, that distorted half of a clock floating around in his vision would drive him nuts.

"I ask you again, who sent you?"

"Your mom. She's very disappointed in the career path you've chosen." Kyle's remaining eye searched for something to look at where the distorted display wouldn't bother him.

Hideki nodded to Diego. The ninja pulled out his machete and walked towards Kyle.

Diego chopped down into the gash on Kyle's arm but the knife still could not break through the reinforced bone.

The modified painkillers in Kyle's system capped the maximum intensity of painful sensations that reached his brain. This prevented the repeated cuts into his body with a machete from causing anything more than mild discomfort. Earlier versions of these drugs had completely numbed the user to all pain, but after several customers died bleeding out from injuries they were unaware of, the formula was changed so that everything produced at least a noticeable amount of feeling.

"I guess this is why you had to sneak up on me, huh?" Kyle looked up and gave a one eyed smile to Diego.

Diego yanked the machete back out of Kyle's arm and wiped the sappy super-oxygenated blood off of it. He brought the machete down again into Kyle's arm.

Again it got stuck.

With a furious battle cry Diego ripped the machete out of Kyle's arm and slammed it back down. The reinforced bone snapped and the machete went all the way through, taking his forearm clean off. The severed hand smacked into the hard floor facing palm up. Deep red blood oozed from stump on Kyle's arm like a spilled bottle of syrup at a pancake joint.

The ninja pulled down his mask, revealing a serious tan line across his eyes, and spit on Kyle. With a confident smile, Diego wiped the blood off his machete and walked back alongside his boss.

Kyle looked down at his severed arm. While it would take a long time for enough of the dense blood in his system to bleed out to the point at which he would die, it was still just a matter of time. The countdown for his escape had begun.

The chain was still around his arm, near his elbow. *What an idiot, you never leave the elbow.* He shook his head in silent disapproval of the ninja's poor technique.

Kyle gave a wide single eyed grin to his captors. He could taste the blood dripping down from the excavated eye socket on his lips.

"Why are you still smiling?" Boss Hideki demanded.

"Because I have a great health plan." Kyle cheerfully replied.

One of the best in the industry in fact! Kyle's company had signed up with Advanced Performance Health, an HMO specializing in quick turn bioprinting and performance enhancing supplements.

"Who else is with you?" Hideki continued to question him.

One of the bodyguards searched through Kyle's shirt and pulled out his phone. He showed it to Hideki and then tossed it back on to the workbench.

"Nobody. Do I look like a person who needs help?" Kyle said as he rattled the chain on his intact arm and shot them an offended look with his remaining eye.

One of the bodyguards whispered in Hideki's ear and he nodded in agreement.

"It would appear you are unwilling to cooperate. When you have changed your mind, tell Marcelo everything you know and he will make things quick for you. If you do not, then I am sure that your suffering will be long and painful."

"I bet." Kyle rolled his lone eye.

Boss Hideki got up from his stool and left the cell with

both bodyguards and the asshole ninja in tow. Diego winked a golden eye at him as he slammed the door shut.

That left Kyle alone with the old torturer. He scanned the room as he planned his escape. No guns, no visible alarm buttons in the cell and no radio or phone visible on Marcelo.

Keys jingled in Marcelo's pocket as he walked over to his workbench and perused all the ways he could cause Kyle great suffering. That was also bad form; a good torturer never left the keys on their body. Kyle shifted to his right a bit to get more slack in the chain on his fully attached arm. He pulled back on his stump until he felt the iron shackle get just above the bleeding end of his arm.

Marcelo picked up what looked like an oversized stainless steel wire cutter from his workbench. Creases formed on his face along the sides of the scar as he grinned at Kyle and walked over.

Kyle pointed his head down at the floor so Marcelo couldn't see his eye. He waited for the old man to get close. Steps echoed off the bare concrete walls of the windowless cell.

The tips of his shoes entered Kyle's vision.

"Let's see that smile again." Marcelo said as he clicked the jaws of the steel pliers in his hand.

Kyle lowered his shortened arm down and the chain slid off on to the floor. Kyle jumped to his feet and stump punched Marcelo in the side of the head. The force of the hit knocked him into grasping range of Kyle's good right arm. He wrapped the loose chain attached to his intact arm around the neck of his would be torturer and fell backwards on to the floor, dragging Marcelo down with him. He pinned Marcelo's body with his massive drug fueled calves and pulled the chain tight around his neck, a position matching the cover of a BDSM movie he had seen advertised in the airport on his way to the Caribbean.

After what looked like two minutes elapsed on his distorted eyes-only display clock, Kyle could no longer feel any twitching from Marcelo and decided that now was a safe time to escape.

Kyle unwound the chain from Marcelo's neck and spun his limp body around to get the keys out of his pocket. Now both arm and stump were free and he was back in business.

He walked over to the workbench and picked up his body armor. Blood stained the crimson panels of the armored shirt. Red shirts were always best for this kind of work, easier to wash afterwards. With some difficulty he managed to get the shirt back on with his one good hand.

Kyle grabbed his phone, which looked remarkably undamaged in its bullet, water and fire proof case. Normally, Kyle would unlock it with his left hand, using the RFID tag printed into it. Fortunately, he had a backup plan for the frequent times when he was missing limbs.

"Cheeseburger time." Kyle said to his phone as he pressed the unlock button and pointed the retina scanner at his remaining eye. The phone unlocked even though only one retina registered, a security issue that had been left in at the behest of various pirate clubs around the world who claimed that a dual retina unlock was discriminatory.

The phone unlocked and reconnected to the eyes only display printed inside of Kyle's remaining eye. The event cell even had an open wireless internet connection available. Presumably so people could send their last emails before having their teeth pulled out, how civilized.

He thumbed through the settings on his phone and flicked the eyes-only display from stereo to monoscopic. His remaining eye stopped twitching around and relaxed once the distorted clock and heading indicators in his field of view were replaced with steady versions made to work with only one eye.

His vision improved and a potential headache avoided, Kyle opened the Instakill app on his phone and took a picture of his newest victim using the camera printed into his eye. After taking the picture Kyle added a tasteful old west color filter to it. He then uploaded the image to his online portfolio on Hitboard along with a hashtag so he could find it later.

#armlessbutnotharmless

He walked towards the workbench and pulled a scalpel off of it. It was sharp but it didn't have much reach. A quick survey of the workbench's contents revealed nothing but short precision instruments. As his gaze dropped back down to the ground, he noticed his severed arm lying on the concrete. That chunk of arm had more reach than any of these surgery tools. Kyle picked up his severed arm and tried to find a good grip that didn't involve holding his own hand.

Armed with his arm and some spare pliers in his pocket he opened the door of the event cell and stepped out.

The next room greeted Kyle with scents of cooking tempura and fish. Warm air in the kitchen enveloped his body and he heard the sizzling tempura being cooked on his blind side. Kyle turned his body towards the sizzling. Two chefs stood frozen next to their steaming woks, their eyes locked on to his. He smiled back at them. The two chefs looked at each other and then one ran screaming out of the building. The other chef snatched his wok off the open flame and rushed at Kyle.

The chef flung the contents of his wok at Kyle. Scalding hot oil and partially cooked shrimp sailed through the air at him. He turned to protect his remaining eye and shielded his head with his good arm. Oil burned the exposed skin on his head and hand. A piece of shrimp bounced off his body armor and his chest heated up as the searing oil soaked through his clothing.

Kyle lowered his arm and spun back around just in time to see the chef swing the scalding hot wok at him. He intercepted the blow with his stump. The hot iron cauterized the open wound quite nicely and added just a hint of sesame oil. Kyle pulled his stump back. The wok, which had fused to his stump, came out of the chef's hands. Without a wok to defend himself with, the chef gasped and stepped back. Kyle closed in, smacking him in the face with his severed hand until the chef was backed into the wall. He then dropped his severed arm and tore the wok off of his stump. He slammed the wok into the side of the chef's head. The impact drove his head into the wall, knocking him out and damaging the part of his brain that contained his secret ramen recipe, which was now lost forever.

Kyle examined the contents of the kitchen but didn't see any cheeseburgers or any other readily edible food anywhere so he headed out. Before he could get to the door, all of the henchmen on the island who Kyle hadn't already killed showed up outside of the kitchen windows and opened fire. Instinctively, Kyle dove for cover beneath the stainless steel tables. As he went down he counted about twenty armed men and women firing at him along with the chef that had run out screaming, who was now trying to figure out how to work the safety on a machine gun.

The explosives in his duffle bag all had remote detonators built into them. He had no idea where they had been taken, but he didn't see them here in the kitchen and they weren't in the event cell, so Kyle fired up the detonator app on his phone and hoped they were still in range as he pressed the 'detonate all' button.

A giant fireball erupted out of the building behind the armed Yakuza The force of the blast knocked all of the goons in the courtyard to the ground as pulverized adobe shot to the sky.

Slowly Kyle peered up through a window to see what had happened. The thugs staggered around as they got back up to their feet. Only dust and the blast wave had reached them. Kyle cursed himself for not detonating the explosives earlier.

Back on their feet, the Yakuza opened fire on the kitchen. A hail of bullets shattered all of the windows and scattered shards of glass across the tables and floor. Knives clanged off of the floor as bullets tore through the racks holding them against the walls. Kyle's reinforced eardrums were put to the test as they dampened the acoustic assault from the echoes rattling throughout the kitchen.

Kyle ducked below the windows and pressed his back to the wall. The goons outside kept shooting, and if they had enough ammo, they'd break through the thin concrete walls soon enough. He looked around the room, taking in the possibilities and muttering to himself.

"Stove, stove, stove. Microwave. Sink. Pots and pans. Come on, Kyle!" A piece of the wall flew away from the window ledge and hit him in the shoulder. "Dammit." He scowled over his shoulder at his attackers, irritated they dared to interrupt his scheming against them. That's when he saw it. Large plastic bins holding chopsticks, forks, knives, and spoons. Soup spoons, teaspoons, and dessert spoons. The boss must have a lot of classy dinner parties on this remote island to need all those spoons. There was even a bin of tiny little spoons Kyle wouldn't know what to do with. He reached over his head and grabbed a bin of silverware. Then another. The silverware clinked against each other and he looked at a fistful of steak knives sitting next to the sink.

Perfect.

Kyle crouched low as he scurried from window to

window, placing fistfuls of cutlery on the ledges. When it was all in place, he pulled the gas lines from the stoves. With these big commercial grade lines, it wouldn't take long to release enough gas to blow everything out of the building. He just needed time to get clear.

Kyle scuttled over to the microwave and opened the door. He tossed one of the tiny spoons inside and set the timer for one minute. Now, he just had to get out of the middle of his building-sized pipe bomb.

He grabbed the door handle to the cell, hoping it was made of sturdier concrete than the kitchen, and yanked it open. Glancing over his shoulder one final time, he saw that a henchman had pointed a grenade launcher at the kitchen. The grenade sailed through an open window and detonated on impact with the wall.

A wall of flames rushed towards Kyle and the blast flung him across the cell, slamming him into the back wall. Fortunately, it also slammed the door shut so that Kyle's landing wasn't immediately followed by a giant fireball and flying silverware.

Kyle shook it off. The clock on his eyes-only display showed that he hadn't been knocked out. The reinforced bones in his head had absorbed the impact and left a nice dent in the wall he collided with. He got to his feet and took a few wobbly steps. He had to twist his neck extra far to make sure that his blindside was ok. Still, by the time he grabbed the warm handle on the cell door, Kyle was confident he'd complete the job.

Kyle opened the cell door to the smoking, blackened

embers of what remained of the kitchen. Through the windows he could see the bodies of the guards outside strewn about the courtyard ground. Steak knives, chopsticks and dessert spoons protruded at odd angles from the skewered corpses. One in particular reminded Kyle of crème brulée and he remembered that he hadn't eaten lunch yet.

He pulled a pair of submachine guns off two corpses with steak knives embedded in their foreheads. Kyle then rolled over a body with several spoons lodged in it and picked up the grenade launcher that had set off the explosion. Using the strap on the grenade launcher, he slung it over his shoulder.

Fully armed he scanned the courtyard and the surrounding balconies for anyone else who might try to get the drop on him. Safe for the moment, he took a few pictures of the punctured henchmen around him and uploaded them to his portfolio.

#putaspooninthemtheyredone

A helicopter approached. Kyle heard the beating sound of the blades getting louder. He still had time.

The helicopter passed over him and approached the landing pad on top of the main building. It had taken Kyle a whole week to track Hideki to this location. There was no way Kyle was going to spend another week searching for him.

With a submachine gun in his hand, Kyle stormed up to the double doors at the front of the building. The doors were barely hanging in place and Kyle could see through several large holes he had made in them. He kicked in the doors and they fell off their hinges into the entryway. The heavy wood cracked as chunks of the doors splintered across the marble floor.

Kyle started to step through the door frame, and promptly ran into the wall on the side of the doorway since he could only see with one eye and had no depth perception.

"Hmm, this may be tricky." Kyle muttered to himself as he stepped to the side and through the doorway.

His boots skidded slightly on the marble floor of the mansion as he ran in. Kyle checked behind the golden iguana statue in the center of the main entrance and found the immediate vicinity empty. Fresh holes from his earlier assault let light in through the walls but housekeeping had already taken care of cleaning up the debris.

Dust blew in through holes in the walls and broken windows. Those windows that were still intact shuddered as the roar of the helicopter got louder. Kyle rushed up the stairs, past portraits of previous clan bosses, and looked down the hallway.

Diego stood defiantly at the opposite end of the hallway with his arms folded. Kyle lifted up the barrel of the submachine gun and struggled to line up the sights with his only remaining eye. The ninja didn't move a muscle. He pulled the trigger. Gunshots echoed off the tile floor of the hallway as the remainder of the clip shredded an ancient vase just behind the ninja.

The ninja shook his head as he looked back over his

shoulder at the pieces of the shattered vase. "I see now that I should have finished you off myself. It was foolish of me to leave you to that old man." Diego pulled out a black machete. "Fortunately, fate has given me another opportunity."

Silent footsteps raced across the tile floor as Diego closed in on him thanks to the custom microstructure of the rubber in the soles of his shoes.

Kyle dropped the empty submachine gun and it clattered off of the floor. He reached around his chest and fumbled for the handle on the grenade launcher. The ninja raised the machete over his head and quietly leapt at Kyle without so much as a grunt. Kyle always found it hard to resist letting out a magnificent battle cry whenever he was about to decapitate someone. Kyle doubted the ninja's true enthusiasm for his job just as his finger found the handle of a grenade launcher.

Frantically, Kyle pulled on the grenade launcher and brought it out in front of him. He glanced down and saw that he was holding it upside down. With a quick flick of his wrist he flipped the grenade launcher up and over. In one fluid motion he grabbed the handle out of the air and brought his finger down on the trigger. The launcher fired a grenade just in front of the leaping ninja. It detonated on impact with the tile floor. The explosion tore the ninja's legs off and bounced the rest of his body off the ceiling. His machete clanged against the tile as it bounced off the floor. The dismembered ninja smacked onto the cold tile with a satisfying splat as paintings crashed off of the walls down the entire length of the hallway.

Kyle aimed the grenade launcher at the helpless ninja. The ceiling shook above him as the helicopter landed. He was out of time. He ran past Diego, kicking him in the face for good measure as he raced by.

At the far side of the hallway, a door led to the roof. Kyle kicked the door but it was locked from the other side. If he kicked it a few more times he could break through, but he didn't have time to waste. Instead, he backed up around a corner and fired another grenade at the door. The blast blew the door off its hinges, sending it and the bodyguard who had been standing behind sailing off of the roof.

Kyle stepped through the smoldering doorway and looked around. Hideki and the two bodyguards who had been with him in the cell were on the edge of the helipad walking towards the helicopter. One of Hideki's bodyguards opened fire at Kyle. Bullets bounced off the edges of the doorway as Kyle fired a grenade at the helicopter.

The explosion from the grenade tore off the landing gear on one side of the helicopter and it lurched over sideways. The blades dug into the roof and the whole aircraft spun around the landing pad like a blender gone mad. Blood splattered across the rooftop as the helicopter blades carved one of the bodyguards in half. The tail rotor came around and shredded the other bodyguard.

Boss Hideki ducked and rolled away from the spinning blades. He had just gotten to his feet when one of the helicopter blades caught on a steel structural beam in the roof and snapped. The composite blade shattered and a large chunk flew towards Hideki. The jagged piece of helicopter blade punched through his eye and out the back of his head. The boss's body went limp and fell backwards on to the rooftop.

The blades of the helicopter ground to a halt. Kyle walked over to survey the damage. The pilot had been killed by the grenade explosion and there didn't appear to be anybody else who was still alive around him. He poked Boss Hideki's body with his boot and was satisfied that the two foot shard of metal that had gone through his head was fatal.

His task completed, Kyle pulled out his phone, linked it to the camera in his remaining eye and took a picture of his eliminated target with his Instakill app. After adding a tasteful starry border and a classy hashtag fitting the demise of a mob boss, he punched the 'Job Complete' button on his phone. With the picture uploaded to the Hitboard server, the contract closed and the hit was added to his resume.

#deathcomesforusallandsometimesithitsyouintheeye

A few seconds later his phone beeped and a green checkbox appeared inside the app. Now he just needed to get back home.

Kyle looked out over the rest of the compound and didn't see anyone. They must have already run away or been killed. No matter, the contract was only for Hideki.

He called up his own helicopter for a pick up. The

headset printed into his ear and the microphone printed inside of his throat automatically connected to his phone.

"Well, you can't really use the landing pad here I kind of blew that up." Kyle said over the phone to the pilot. "What? You want me to walk all the way back down to the end of the driveway? That's like a mile from here." Kyle complained as he looked out at the beach on the backside of the main compound. "Hey, how about you pick me up on the beach on the south side? I'm already right next to it. I can get there in a few minutes."

Kyle hopped off the top of the building down to the ground below. His enhanced muscles and bones absorbed the impact from the fall and he left a six inch deep divot in the soft soil. The outer fence on this side of the compound was a meager chain link affair. There didn't appear to be any security systems here at all, no cameras or automated turrets or anything. Maybe if he had come from this direction in the first place he wouldn't have been caught by that asshole ninja. It certainly looked easier.

The helicopter touched down at the far end of the beach just before the waterline and Kyle jogged over to it. He was almost home; soon he would have a new arm and eye along with his traditional celebratory cheeseburger to commemorate a job well done.

Click!

Kyle froze in place and looked down. There was something very hard buried in the sand underneath his left foot.

Suddenly the lack of security on this side of the island

made a lot more sense. He redialed the helicopter pilot. "Hey, I'm going to need some help up. I just stepped on a land mine."

"Again?" He had used this pilot before.

"Yes, again." Kyle replied, annoyed at this new inconvenience. Getting blown up by a mine always sucked. "Can you please have the bags ready?"

"Yeah, you got it. Just like last time. You gotta be more careful about these things, you know?"

"Yeah, I know. But they always put me back together so no biggie."

"You're not the one who has to spend twenty minutes picking up the little bits afterwards."

"Oh, quit whining. You get overtime pay for that right?"

"True." The pilot, like any good mercenary, never turned down an opportunity for some overtime.

"Good, then you can thank me later." Kyle hung up and stepped off the mine.

The explosion propelled him upwards and he saw his legs fly past him as everything faded to black.

CHAPTER THREE

An electric shock through his fingertips jolted Kyle awake.

"Ow! What the hell?" Kyle shouted. His head jumped up as he was jolted awake. He looked around trying to figure out where he was. Wait, no, he had two eyes now. He closed one eye and then the other. Yes, both were in and working. They had probably given him another green one. That was disappointing. He had been hoping to try a mismatched pair on his next hospital trip, to follow the latest fashion trend.

The hospital Kyle was in had several Winston-Salem BioIndustries Limbscaper GX5925 bioprinters in the basement. These were top of the line machines that could print a whole arm in just a few hours and eyes even quicker. Kyle was a frequent customer so they kept cartridges pre-filled with his cells on ice to speed up recovery time by avoiding the need to grow new cell cultures from scratch. Using cells from the patient removed the risks of rejection and had put a serious damper on the international organ trade. The Limbscaper GX5925 also featured the ability to lay down layers of copper and other metals along with cells. Electronics like the camera in Kyle's eyes were printed in with the rest of the organ as they built up everything layer by layer, avoiding the mess and hassle of implants.

Kyle relaxed his head back down into the pillow. He had made it home safely.

"Ah, good, I see the new nerves were connected properly. Good morning. I'm Nurse Steve. I'm going to run a sensory test on each of your new fingers and your palm. You should feel six shocks."

Six more mild electric shocks pricked into each of Kyle's fingers and the palm of his new left hand. These shocks felt stronger than the ones they usually used, this nurse must have cranked up the settings. The new hand was still locked into a dull gray plastic scaffold attached to the end of his arm. This kept the newly grafted limb in place. Similar scaffolds covered his legs. The nurse shocked each of his toes to confirm that both legs had been attached properly.

His right arm had survived the explosion from the land mine and aside from some singed skin it looked just like how Kyle last saw it, tan and smooth, without a single body hair on it.

Like all people who could afford it, Kyle took pills to safely tan without the need for dangerous UV exposure and to prevent unwanted body hair from growing in the first place. A special accessory cream was required for any areas where hair was still desired, like the top of his head.

"And you can see out both eyes? No distortion or color blindness?" Nurse Steve asked as he waved a mini flashlight in front of Kyle's eyes.

"Yeah, I can see fine. My eyes only display is off though. Do you have my phone?"

"Yes, let me get your things for you. You have some visitors as well." Nurse Steve pulled the flashlight away. He released the clamps on the scaffolds, pulled them off Kyle's arm and legs, placed them on a cart and left the room. Fortunately for Kyle, this hospital took great pride in their ability to perfectly match new limbs to the patient's body

Kyle brought his new arm up to his face for closer inspection.

They hadn't tanned it to match!

His new arm was a freshly bioprinted shade of pale and a distinct line was visible on his forearm where the artificially tanned skin met the new limb. Kyle pulled up the bedsheets and leaned forward to take a closer look at his new legs. They were both pale too! It looked like he had been wearing uneven knee high socks outside for months.

Had the hospital run out of melanin cartridges for their printers? He gazed around the room and realized that he wasn't in his usual recovery suite either. He had been woken up in a standard dull gray hospital room without even a TV to keep him company. What was going on?

The door to his room opened and Kira Faizal stepped in. She wore a black and orange motorcycle jacket over a purple tank top. Black shoulder length hair draped over the shoulders of her jacket and a bright orange highlight ran along the tips. Bronze olive skin that resulted from the mixture of her Thai and Persian blood peeked out from the midriff between the tank top and her jeans, giving a sneak peek at abs strong enough to give herself an abortion.

Not that she would ever need one. Like most women who could afford to, Kira had already had her ovaries removed to prevent unwanted pregnancies and periods from getting in the way of her daily life. Most typically got their ovaries removed during high school or college and fresh ones printed and put back in when they decided the time was right to start a family. This of course led to outrage from various religious groups complaining that printing new ovaries when it was convenient led to sexual promiscuity even though they reduced the need for abortions, which those same groups also complained about.

"Hi Kyle. New limbs feeling ok?" Kira asked. She sipped on a cup of coffee as she sat down in the lone chair in the room next to his bed. The leather in her jacket made a scrunching noise as she eased into her seat.

"Yeah, they work alright, but for some reason they didn't tan them to match." Kyle said as he pushed the button on the side of the bed to lift himself into a seated position. "I guess it could be worse. The tanning pills will take care of these in a few weeks."

"That's good." Kira took another sip of coffee as she examined him. "Tell me Kyle, do you know why you keep getting caught and injured this badly? The helicopter pilot delivered you in stasis bags this time. You're lucky your head didn't get blown apart by that explosion."

"I don't know. It doesn't matter as long the job gets done right?" Kyle furrowed his brow as he tried to read Kira's expression.

"To a degree." Kira's eyes remained focused on his. "I remember when you were just a tall, lanky sniper that I recruited for your aim and cleverness. Your rifle has been sitting in my closet for years by the way. You seem to keep forgetting to pick it up."

"Ha." Kyle shrugged. "Back then I was just a wuss who couldn't strike fear into anyone. I had to hide and snipe at them since I couldn't get close enough to do any real damage."

"I see." Kira looked down at her cup of coffee and took a long swig of it.

The door to the room opened again and this time a salt and pepper haired, half-Spanish and half-Russian man entered. A thin beard and even thinner mustache adorned his leathery face. Vitron Demenska, Kyle's boss, didn't do get well visits, which meant he was here on business.

Vitron had created the world famous Demenska technique. The assassin stabbed a knife through the bottom of the target's jaw. The knife had to be a long thin blade rigid enough to slide through the upper palate. This bypassed any potentially reinforced bones in the facial structure and went straight into the target's brain. Death came instantly and quietly.

Avery, Vitron's human resources manager, followed him into the room and took up a position against the far wall. As the only person in the entire organization who had never killed anyone, Avery had no need for combat enhancing drugs but the half Jamaican and half Taiwanese woman did take some cosmetic pills, including those for her hair. Ultraviolet reactive pigmentation in her long hair allowed her to look like a professional during the day and an anime character at night when she went out dancing. She clutched a tablet against her chest and avoided making eye contact with Kyle as she walked in.

"Hey guys." Kyle waved to his new visitors. "You're all here. Thanks for coming by. Avery, do you know what's up with the printers here? They didn't tan my new limbs to match."

"Kyle." Avery paused and took a deep breath. She tightened the grip on her tablet and turned her head up to face Kyle. "Your limbs don't match because we reduced your insurance coverage prior to the change." She let out a deep exhale and attempted to smile at him.

"What change? Why? What's going on?" Kyle searched Avery and Kira's faces for answers. He found them both looking towards Vitron.

Vitron walked up to Kyle and put his hand on the side of the bed. His wedding ring clinged against the metal rail. Vitron was single, but he wore the ring to help attract his preferred kind of women. It also served as an explosive device if he ever found himself in an unpleasant situation.

Vitron looked up and down Kyle's body and shook his head. He straightened his back and forced a smile.

"Kyle." Vitron spoke slowly, carefully selecting every word. "You have been getting very sloppy lately."

Kyle started to say something, but Vitron put up his hand to stop him.

"No, let me talk first. You have been causing way too much collateral damage, to other people, to the environment and to yourself. Do you remember Burkina Faso?"

"Yeah, I remember." Kyle vividly remembered his mission to the small African nation to take out the prince, son of the reigning king, whom many did not want to succeed to the throne. To this day Kyle was still impressed by the size and forest like density of the prince's beard. "That prince had a huge beard, thick too. He…"

"Do you remember," Vitron cut him off and looked at him sternly, "how you killed over fifty people in a very public space in order to take him out?"

"I was in a hurry. There was a playoff game starting like an hour after that and I didn't want to miss it." Kyle protested.

"There you go again." Vitron shook his head. "Always in a rush, never taking into consideration the details and subtleties that are so important in our line of work. These past few years, you have lost your tact. When you first started working for me, you used to sneak in and take out a target without the person next to them even noticing. Now you storm around blowing everything up with all the subtlety of an air raid. I don't know if you can even hit a single target anymore without using a grenade launcher."

Kyle decided not to bring up his choice of weapon after his eye got plucked out at Hideki's compound.

"I thought sending you to an island in the middle of nowhere would be good for you, that it would be an ideal case where you could cause all the damage you wanted without any problems. But instead you got caught, again. How sad is that? And then you step on a landmine on your way out, again, and we have to replace a bunch of your limbs, again. Do you see the problem here for us? It's sloppy and amateurish and it keeps happening. You have turned into one of those idiot NASCAR rookies who actively cause accidents because they know someone will put them back together afterwards."

Kyle's face flushed red as he tried to come up with a counterargument.

"But I always got the target. Isn't that what the most important thing is?"

Vitron glared at him, then sighed and shook his head as he got to the point. "You are costing us too much in respect and you are making our insurance premiums too high."

Kyle's eyes jumped to Avery at the word 'insurance'. Suddenly he knew why she was here. She nodded to him, confirming his suspicions.

"Do you know how much it costs to replace all these parts you keep losing? You haven't made it back from a mission fully intact in years."

"But I thought we were covered for all that?" Kyle asked.

"We are, but our rate is dependent on how often we use it. If you lose a hand or eye here and there on the job, it's no problem, it happens to everyone. But you have had almost every part of your body replaced at least three times. It would have been cheaper for me to clone you, but then I would have to wait for the other you to grow up and hire a nanny and all that." Vitron forced a chuckle.

Kyle just stared at him, his mouth open.

"We are all on the same plan, they charge all of us on the likelihood that one of us will need replacement parts and you have been screwing up the premiums for everyone with your sloppy approach to your work." Vitron continued.

"But aren't we paying to use those replacements? We have to get our money's worth don't we?" Kyle argued back.

"No, this is insurance. You are supposed to pay for it so that you don't have to use it."

"What the fuck does that mean?" Kyle raised his voice. Vitron lifted his hand again and waited for him to calm back down.

"You have had every part of your body replaced except for your head, and that is probably just because they can't print minds into brain tissue yet or I am sure you would have found a way to get that blown off too."

"You could have at least tanned my arm and legs to match. I'm going to look like I love playing soccer in the summer for weeks while they blend in." Kyle complained, hoping for one last chance at getting the benefits he was used to.

"No, that costs extra and we have already spent enough

on you." Vitron looked down at Kyle. "I am afraid that we are going to have to let you go. You are just costing us too much in both money and respect." Vitron sighed a breath of relief as he finished this sentence. He had aired all of his grievances and was no longer worried about Kyle's reaction. Vitron never liked firing an employee but considering it had only taken him a few lifts of his hand to quiet Kyle down, this time had gone rather well. He wouldn't need the knife or the gun under his coat after all.

"You're firing me?" Kyle's eyes bulged open. He glanced towards Avery but she just nodded her head so he looked back to Vitron. His jaw hung open in disbelief.

"Well, I was trying to put it in nicer terms but yes, you're fired." Vitron stated. "Avery will help you with filling out the paperwork to make it official. I will be a reference for you if you need it. But right now you need to focus on cleaning up your act before anyone will want to hire you."

"Would you take me back if I can do that?" Kyle asked hopefully.

"No promises." Vitron said. "But anything is possible. It is up to you what happens. You were one of the best once, I think that is still somewhere inside you if you bother to look. Despite all the problems you have caused us, it has been a pleasure working with you."

Vitron put out his hand.

"Thanks, for everything." Kyle shook Vitron's hand. He was still in a daze as Vitron walked out of the room.

"Are you ready?" Avery asked as she turned on her tablet and walked towards him. Kira remained silent in her chair. She scrutinized him with her eyes.

Kyle had been conscious for less than an hour and already he had discovered that not all of his limbs matched the rest of his body and been fired. Today was not off to a good start.

"Sure, I'm ready to get fired." Kyle said as he fell back deep into the hospital bed.

"Actually, this is called getting laid off." Avery corrected him as she continued preparing documents on her tablet.

"I'm not getting laid, I'm getting fucked. Let's at least be honest about this." Frustration seeped out of Kyle's voice. Avery shook her head and remained calm. She knew he wouldn't try anything with Kira present.

"Please sign this with a retina scan. Either eye will do." She handed him the tablet and he looked at the target in the middle until it turned green. "Great. That confirms that even though your employment has ended the NDA you signed is still in effect and you won't tell anyone what Earthen Home Pottery really does."

Vitron's assassination company masqueraded as a high end pottery shop that only allowed people into the gallery by appointment. Vitron had always been fascinated with pottery and frequently made bowls to relax. He encouraged his subordinates to do the same and put the best pieces in the public facing windows below the main office. None of Kyle's pieces had ever made it to the windows.

Kyle handed the tablet back to her.

"I'm also setting your Hitboard account back to 'Freelancer'." Avery said as she made a few quick presses on her tablet. "This way other companies will know you are looking for a job and any hits you do in the meantime will be credited solely to you."

This was the first time Kyle had ever been a freelancer on Hitboard. He started to wonder how much of an increase in pay per hit he would get without Vitron taking his cut off the top.

"Before you woke up we put you on a reduced plan. That's why your arms didn't get color matched. You should thank Vitron for waiting to do it until all your limbs had been printed. On this new plan you can only get one limb replacement every six months."

"That's it? I go through at least one limb every month when I'm working." Kyle said.

"Yes Kyle, that's exactly why we're letting you go." Avery paused for a moment and looked at Kyle probingly. "Now you have two options for health insurance going forward. You can keep the reduced plan or you can forego that and sign up with another private company of your choice."

"Which way is the quickest?" Kyle didn't like reading insurance forms any more than Vitron did.

"COBRA, you keep the plan you've got but you pay one-hundred and two percent of what we had been paying for you."

"What's with the extra two percent?"

"Administrative costs."

"What? Are they like part time accountants that they only pick up off the street whenever someone gets fired?"

Kyle sensed he should be angry about something but he wasn't sure what. Unable to get properly angry, he remained confused.

"Maybe. I don't know. But you'll keep your current plan, except that the state doesn't cover performance enhancing or cosmetic pills."

"But what about the cheeseburger pills?" Kyle asked with the same level of seriousness that a child uses when he asks about the location of an ice cream truck.

"The ones that convert fat into muscle? Those are both performance enhancing and cosmetic, so no."

"What! But I love cheeseburgers! How much is it to get them directly? Can I just re-add them?" Kyle leaned over to look at the tablet. The bed started to tip over and he recoiled back.

"If you want to do that, you can, but you'll have to start all over as an individual. Here are the rates." She handed Kyle the tablet with the cost sheet for individuals to buy pills a la carte displayed. Kyle's head sank back down into the sheets on his bed, his eyes wide. "These things are custom matched to your genome so you can't just use generics, that's part of why they cost so much."

"Holy shit! No way they cost that much. That's more than ten times what the company was paying. This is almost as much as my yearly mortgage. What gives?"

"If you are out of network they charge you more." Avery said.

"How does that make sense? It's not like I'm using anything else. It costs them the same." Kyle gave up. "Fine.

Let's just leave it. It's not like I'll need them while I'm not working anyway."

"Ok, if you ever have any questions, feel free to contact me at any time. I'll have the nurse bring up your clothes and other things." As Avery finished she stood up and put out her hand to give Kyle a handshake which he respectfully accepted. "It's been a pleasure working with you Kyle."

"Pleasure working with you too." Kyle replied, dumbstruck by what had just happened.

Avery closed up her tablet and left the room. Kira finished up her coffee and tossed it into the trashcan next to her chair.

"You should take some time to consider your options. Not many people get a chance for a clean escape from this business and you just got one." Kira said.

"You say that like I should be happy about this." Kyle stared up at the ceiling.

"Just think about it. I've been doing this for so long I don't know what would happen to me if I got out of it." Kira looked over the vital signs indicators and the hospital bed. "But if you want help getting a new job, just let me know. By the way, when was the last time you took any of the pills?"

"About two weeks ago, right before I left for the assignment. Why?"

"Kyle those pills are going to start wearing off soon. If you want to stay in good enough shape to get a job, you'll need to start eating better and going to a gym."

"What, go to the gym like some damn hippie? Screw that." Kyle's face contorted into a look of disgust. Going to a gym had been beneath him for nearly twenty years. "If they haven't worn off already, maybe they'll last a while longer. I've been taking them for over a decade, I've probably got some excess built up in my system."

"Yeah, well, once you decide what you want to do. Let me know."

"Thanks Kira, I will." Kira walked out, leaving Kyle alone in the room.

CHAPTER FOUR

Kyle took a cab home from the hospital. Each autonomous cab was assigned a unique personality and accent in order to simulate the ancient tradition of random humans shuttling strangers around a city in exchange for fares. This cab was named Margaret and sounded like a southern Belle. As Margaret pulled up to Kyle's building, the AI confirmed the GPS coordinates were correct and the laser, radar, and ultrasonic sensor grids emanating from the car determined that Kyle's building was very tall.

"Wow, who'd you have to kill to get a place like that?" The car asked as Kyle stepped out of it.

"A lot." Kyle answered dryly as he grabbed his bag off the seat. He closed the door before Margaret could download a witty response from the dispatch server.

Kyle breathed in the cool afternoon air. The paired scents of biodiesel and urine mixed in with the cool breeze. He was back home in San Francisco.

His apartment building, a forty story skyscraper, towered over the neighboring four story building. It was the last of the skyscrapers to have been approved in the city over fifty years ago, back when the population was still increasing. Solar cells embedded in the window glass glimmered emerald green in the sunlight. A live human guard, the prized indicator that you were entering a classy joint, waved to Kyle as he walked inside. Kyle waved back to him with his new pale arm. The guard stared quizzically at him as he entered the building. The security system detected the access card in his pocket and automatically called down an elevator for him. The button for his floor illuminated as he entered the elevator.

"Fired." He muttered to himself, still in disbelief. He had been working the same job for almost twenty years. The elevator doors opened at the thirty-eighth floor. Kyle walked out and around the corner to his apartment. Part of the appeal of this location had been that there was no direct line of sight to the elevator. If you wanted to see what was inside the apartment you had to get close. He walked to his door and paused for a second.

"This sucks, I can't believe this." Kyle cursed softly to himself. His mind tried to jump in a hundred directions at once but he caught himself after a few seconds of near panic. Vitron was right, maybe once he calmed down this could be a good opportunity for him.

He pressed his right hand against the wall a few inches away from the doorframe. After a few seconds the sensor hidden in the wall recognized the RFID tag printed into his hand and emitted two beeps signaling that the alarm system and explosives in the door had been disarmed. Satisfied that his apartment wouldn't try to kill him, he brought his wallet closer to the keycard panel on the door to unlock it and walked inside.

The condo was a large one bedroom with a kitchen that faced the living room, an office and a master bedroom with a single bathroom that you had to go through the bedroom to get to. The entry doorway led into the hallway separating the living room from the office and the bedroom, a diabolical T intersection that made getting any furniture in or out of the apartment a frustrating if not impossible task. Aside from the carpet in the bedroom the rest of the apartment had all tile floors to go with the granite countertops in his kitchen, which was spotless from lack of use. The only piece of equipment regularly used in it was the drone delivery landing pad built into one of the kitchen walls that allowed automated delivery drones to drop off food, socks and other supplies vital to survival without the need for exposure to sunlight or other people.

The living room was for public view and innocuous looking. Electrically tintable floor to ceiling windows let lots of light in over his couch and love seat when the fog didn't cover the building. The two pieces of furniture faced a coffee table sitting in front of a rather large TV with a full surround sound system that wirelessly connected to speakers mounted on the side of the kitchen counter.

A false bottom underneath the couch concealed a shotgun with explosive rounds. A normal person would need an axe to get it out, but with the strength enhancing pills Kyle was taking he could smash through the hardwood

45

cover as if it were balsa wood.

The kitchen was similarly tame aside from some grenades Kyle kept in his spice rack that slid out of the base of the counter and the silenced pistol hidden in between the gap between his fridge and the wall. He didn't host many parties.

Down the hallway in the other direction just before the bedroom was a locked office where Kyle kept all his work related equipment. He opened it with another hidden sensor panel and peeked briefly inside to make sure everything was just as he left it. Tablet still plugged in, check. 3D printer with knife edge grade titanium loaded into it, check. Drawer full of knives, unopened, check. Pair of silenced handguns, check. Submachine gun with silencer and mini-rocket launcher attachment, check. Girl Scout cookie box filled with mines, check. Girl Scout cookie box filled with cookies, check. Various body armors, vests and formal attire on the coat rack, check. Punch card for Kokumi Burger, his favorite cheeseburger place, still on his desk with one punch to go until a free burger, delicious check.

He closed the office and walked into his bedroom. The tile gave way to light blue carpet that covered his bedroom floor. The bed called to him to take a nap but he resisted the urge. A shower would be better to clear his head and to wash off the hospital room smell that had followed him home.

Kyle closed his eyes and let the water run down over his newly attached limbs. His new arm and legs looked like they belonged to an albino. He traced a finger over the joint trying to feel a seam between the old and new flesh. Normally he couldn't even tell where to look except for when he got his arm blown off after getting a tattoo. Ink isn't part of your genetic makeup and now all that remained of a formerly bitchin' dragon tattoo on his left arm was just the left eye and part of the face that ended in an abrupt line six inches up from his elbow.

He stepped out of the shower and shook his head as he looked at his two tone body. At least it would even out in a few weeks after the tanning pills kicked in. Speaking of which, he opened up his pill cabinet.

It was empty.

"Of course." Kyle sighed in frustration. He had taken the rest of his pills with him on his business trip to make sure he didn't run out mid-assignment. Only the boxes with the refill numbers on them remained. He grabbed the boxes and ran back for his phone. It had been less than a day, maybe they hadn't processed the reduction in benefits yet.

He fired up the insurance company website and typed in the refill numbers and after each one he was greeted with the same message saying his number was invalid and he needed a new prescription. Those bastards were quick.

Kyle drifted to his couch and dropped himself on to it. In the twenty minutes the shower had taken his mind had suddenly gotten very empty. He had no plans, no upcoming assignments, no weapons to train with, no languages to try to learn, no plane tickets to buy, nothing.

The freedom of having nothing to do overwhelmed him and he sat motionless while all the thoughts about work flowed out and all the possibilities for his newfound freedom swept in.

He was on vacation.

Vacation.

Vacation!

He rolled the word back in forth in the freshly emptied parts of his brain a few more times. The word brought a smile back to his face.

Kyle had been working continuously ever since he got out of community college and enlisted with the marines. It had been years since he had gone more than two weeks without anyone trying to kill him. This wouldn't be so bad. Nearly two decades of work as a hired gun had left Kyle with a fair bit of cash and now he suddenly found himself with time to enjoy it.

He grabbed his tablet out of his office and checked his overseas bank account. There was enough money in there for him to last at least a year with his current mortgage. He could take a few months off without any issues. That would be a good break, long enough for him to relax, but not so long that he would lose his edge.

The vacation started now, he declared silently to himself. But what would be the best way to start it off?

A fancy burger and a night at the club followed by some casual sex with a stranger would be the perfect way to get over being fired.

Kyle browsed the most expensive cheeseburger locations

in the city looking for one that was near a nightclub. He selected a burger joint in the Marina district at the north end of town. Even for San Francisco it was a wealthy area, sure to be filled with artificially modelesque physiques. He would fit in perfectly and the selections of meat for dessert would be just as good as what he got for dinner.

Kobe beef is a heavily marbled fatty type of beef. First recognized in Japan in 1943 as a type coming from Wagyu cattle in the Kobe prefecture of Japan, for over a hundred years it had been celebrated as one of the finest types of meat around. In the American tradition of continual improvement through excess, the Kobe beef patty in the cheeseburger Kyle had just ordered at Beefpura arrived wrapped in bacon, covered in panko breadcrumbs, sandwiched between slices of smoked Gouda and deep fried. The crunching noise from biting into it was loud and satisfying, the crispy outside contrasted well against the melt in your mouth softness of the meat within.

The night was off to a good start.

Satisfied with a delicious meal, Kyle set off towards the club across the street. Green lasers projected the Helix Power logo on to a wall of slowly rising fog above the entrance. The laser and fog machine were self-contained and easily reconfigurable. This made it easy to change the logo when the venue failed every other year and the owners had to re-open it under a new name to avoid paying their taxes and creditors.

In this meat market of a club, Kyle was a piece of drug enhanced Kobe beef. A typical night out involved getting himself a drink and then skirting the outside of the dance floor to look for an equally well enhanced woman to make eye contact with. The two of them would then head out to the dance floor to engage in the pre-game ritual of feeling each other up to make sure that their bodies were as good as they looked and that neither was some poser trying to fake that they were on the good drugs. If things went well he would head home with them. If things went very well he would head home to their place and avoid the awkward conversation about why he had two security systems on his door and a locked office. If things went exceptionally well he might even buy them a drink.

"Hey bro, do you lift?" Asked a man with a blue quarter Mohawk standing between him and the bar.

"Of course not. Do you?" Kyle responded as he tried to determine if he could get a free drink out of this.

"Ha, hell no. What do I look like? A poser?" The man cheerfully slapped Kyle on the shoulder and walked away towards the dance floor.

An electronic remix of A Drop of Light's fifty year old classic 'This Heart is Mine' blared over the speakers as Kyle ordered a drink off the touchscreen enabled counter top of the bar. Within moments a circle appeared on the counter with his name flashing inside of it. Kyle pressed his thumb against his name and sensors below the counter confirmed his order, payment method and current blood alcohol level. The circle slid open and his drink rose up from the machinery below.

At the far end of a bar a woman undressed Kyle with the

ultrasonic implants in her silver eyes. Kyle perked one of his eyebrows in her direction and gestured with his head for her to come over as he grabbed his drink. Her eyes paused on his crotch as they switched back to the visible spectrum and she caught sight of his mismatched hands. The woman turned up her nose and shook her head as she walked away from him.

No biggie, Kyle told himself, her loss. He just had to find somebody who was into mismatched body parts.

Drink in hand, Kyle proceeded to walk the perimeter of the dance floor. The crowd flowed around the multitude of structural pylons that jutted up through the floor at odd angles as they came and went. One woman attempted to pole dance around a two foot thick concrete pillar, much to her friends' delight. Kyle drifted along the walls, occasionally ducking underneath a beam as he scoped out the local wildlife.

He passed a man and a woman who were staring at each other's foreheads as they talked to each other. The social warfare apps on their phones had picked up the facial recognition scans from their eye cameras and were now projecting any publicly available info they could find about the other person along with any common connections into their field of view.

"Hey, weren't you at the party with Fila?" The woman asked the man as her eyes went back and forth across the text in her vision. "I used to live with a friend of one of her former coworkers."

"Oh yeah, that was Livani right?" The man nodded as he

glanced at the wall behind her to get a clearer look at the results that had shown up in his HUD. "Yeah, I went to school with one of her old boyfriend's former neighbors. Wow, we're really close."

Kyle rolled his eyes and continued on.

Half way around the room Kyle's eyes met the iridescent gray and blue eyes of a woman wearing a teal tube top beneath a fuzzy orange quarter jacket. She was dancing just outside a large circle of people. Mismatched eyes, she had beaten him to the latest fashion trend, with any luck she would appreciate mismatched skin as well.

The woman turned her body towards him and batted her eyelashes. Kyle lifted one of his in response. She nodded and Kyle reached into his pocket and tapped his phone to run his social warfare app on her. It was dark in the club but the random flashes of light off her face were enough to capture a good scan.

The facial recognition check came back negative. Kyle had never seen this woman before and she wasn't in the Hitboard database either. She wouldn't have any bad memories of him and she probably wouldn't try to kill him either.

Kyle downed the rest of his drink and walked over to the woman. The speakers were pointed down at the dance floor and the volume of the music increased to near deafening levels as he approached.

"Hi, I'm Kyle." He shouted into her ears, barely able to make out his own words.

"I'm Richelle Ratulangi." Richelle yelled back into Kyle's

ear. "What flavors are you packing big guy?"

Like all men with the means to afford it, Kyle had replaced his testicles with custom printed ones that featured built in birth control. They still produced testosterone to keep his body chemically in balance, but the sperm they produced were all duds. High end testicle specific printers, such as the DaddyStopper 9 that printed Kyle's balls, could even add artificial colors and flavoring.

"Lemon and lime." Kyle screamed into her ears. He held up his unmatched hands. "You seem like a girl who likes a good combination."

"You're right about that." Kyle felt her hands run down his chest as she wrapped one of her legs around one of his. She winked at him with her gray eye. Her lips were a few inches below Kyle's and covered in metallic dark blue lip gloss. Kyle considered that he might have to buy this girl a drink but decided to start with light conversation.

"That's quite a name. Where are you from?" Kyle yelled at her face.

"Here, but my dad is from Indonesia and my mom is from Pakistan."

"Your dad is from Afghanistan? That's awesome! I've been there! I'm Samoan." The music got even louder.

"Oh, I love Samoas! Those are my favorite kind of Girl Scout cookie!"

"You were a Girl Scout! That's hot!" Kyle screamed back at her.

Richelle grabbed both of his butt cheeks. Like a true professional Kyle winked at her and then flexed each cheek individually to demonstrate the control he possessed over his body. Richelle sank her hands into his back pockets and stood on her tiptoes. She stretched her face up towards his, puckering with eyes half closed. Kyle bent his head to hers and their lips met. Soft. Warm. Moist, with a hint of metal.

"You wanna get out of here?" Kyle shouted seductively at her left ear.

Richelle nodded her head and they went outside.

"So where's your place at?" Richelle asked. Kyle silently cursed on the inside. He was going to have to explain why he had two alarm systems again. At least they had left before he had needed to buy her a drink.

"In SoMa, in a high rise. Thirty-eighth floor." Kyle responded with a grin.

"Ooh, hard bodied and wealthy. I'm glad you didn't spend everything on that hot body of yours." She licked her blue lips.

Kyle was thankful that Richelle didn't question why he had to use two different locks to enter his apartment. Once the door closed she grabbed Kyle's neck and leapt on to him, wrapping her brown leather boots around his body. He slipped his hands under her jacket and slid it off as she leaned backwards off his chest. While he held her up she pulled her tube top off revealing the two small breasts that adorned her drug-toned chest. A single large feather tattoo curved in between them. Not a single tan line was visible anywhere. She definitely had access to the good pills.

Kyle walked her to his bedroom and threw her on to the bed. He pulled off his diamond textured red polo shirt and tossed his silver jeans in a corner. For now he left his black silk boxers on, to maintain some mystery. At the same time, Richelle pulled both of her boots off and dropped them next to Kyle's bed.

"Nice striping." Richelle said as she admired the two shades of color on Kyle's arm. "I like how you had the tattoo artist make that dragon look like it was cut off below the eye."

"Oh yeah, that was totally the idea." Kyle said as he gazed down at her.

"Turn the light off." Kyle tossed one of her boots at the light switch and left them only with the stray moonlight coming in through the cracks of his bedroom window.

Richelle giggled as he kissed her stomach and worked his way down to her hips. With a flick of his wrist the buttons on her skirt detached and he spun her around as he took it off.

A dull green glow arose from Richelle's crotch and radiated across the entire room, coating everything in a pale neon green hue.

"Um, are you glowing?" Kyle asked.

"I like to think of it as fairies in my secret garden. I had them tone down the brightness so you can only see it when the lights are off."

"Whoa, very cool." Kyle had never seen bioluminescent pubic hair before.

Bioluminescent hair was another fashion trend Kyle had yet to try out. Assassins typically avoided any enhancements that made them more visible at night.

Musicians on the other hand often made the hair on their heads glow. Occasionally they would also add the effect to their chests to increase power of a dramatic shirt ripping finale. Polish punk rocker Bartek Rudzielec famously applied the effect to his back hair, which he had shaved into the shape of glowing red bat wings.

Richelle raised her legs and moved them so that her knees were on top of Kyle's shoulders. The glow of her crotch illuminated his face.

"Blow the glow baby." Richelle said.

Kyle got down on his knees, happy to oblige.

CHAPTER FIVE

A loud noise disturbed Kyle's slumber. He rolled over to try and block the noise with his pillow but the sound kept getting louder and louder. His arms itched as they slid against the fabric of his pillow. That was very annoying and didn't help him get back to sleep either.

The noise continued to increase in volume despite Kyle's best efforts to ignore it. Slowly, he rolled back towards the harsh screeching. His chest and legs also itched as he shifted his body around. A green light shone through the skin of his eyelids. There was going to be no sleeping through this.

"What?" Kyle groggily asked as he slowly opened his eyes. "Why are you yelling?"

"You know fucking well why you damn poser!" Richelle screamed at him. She stood naked beside Kyle's bed. The glow from her pubes illuminated the bottom of her throat and shifted around the room as she gestured wildly, yelling at him like a mad lighthouse in the night.

"What are you talking about?" Kyle grumbled as his eyes

struggled to adjust to the rapidly fluctuating light. "Why are you even still here? And why am I all itchy?"

Typically if he woke up itching after sleeping with someone he had to get a different set of pills and he wasn't sure if COBRA covered those.

"You know damn well why you're itchy you bastard!" She stormed over to the other side of the bedroom and turned on the ceiling light. An even fluorescent hue diffused over the entire room and replaced the shifting green glow. "You lied to me! You can't afford any of the good pills! You were just faking it to get me in bed! Just look at yourself!"

"What the hell are you talking about?" He rubbed his eyes and looked down at his chest. Where six pack abs had been the day before was now a lump of flab with hundreds of tiny hairs springing back to life all over it.

Kyle shrieked and fell backwards out of his bed.

He jolted to his feet and examined his body. All over his skin tiny little body hairs that had been suppressed for decades struck back at him. He had to fight to keep his fingers from scratching all over his body.

His eyes locked on his chest and opened wide. The cheeseburger pills, his favorite ones of all, had abandoned him as well. He lightly tapped his bulging stomach. It jiggled. He never jiggled.

He screamed.

Kyle grabbed a hold of his flabby stomach and pulled on it. It was like he had woken up in someone else's body. He tried to suck in his gut to see if he could make it go away but it came back every time he exhaled.

The rest of his body had gotten flabbier as well. The bottoms of his arms sagged as he flailed around. He grabbed on to his head to try and calm himself down but felt the hair at the front of his scalp slide off underneath his fingers. Kyle looked down in terror at the wads of hair sitting on his now flabby fingers.

"I don't even see any Samoas here! Was that a lie too or did your fat ass eat them all?" Richelle yelled as she put her clothes back on.

"What the hell are you talking about? I am Samoan!" Kyle shouted back.

"And I'm hurt." Richelle said dramatically as she put her hands over her heart.

"Wait, I think we have something of a misunderstanding going here." Kyle replied with a trembling voice.

"Yeah, you bet we fucking do. I thought you were real. I was ready to add you to my rotation. But instead you're just another poser renting some rich guy's place to trick people like me who are out of your league." She growled as she forced her tube top back on.

Kyle froze in place as he tried to process everything that was happening. He looked down at his new gut. Then he stared at the hair in his hands. A moment later itching all over his body interrupted him. After some frantic scratching he was back to gazing down at the flab on his stomach.

The doorbell rang.

"Who the hell is that?" Kyle wondered aloud. It was

early in the morning and nobody had called to get buzzed in.

"Probably the owner of this place coming to kick your cheap renter ass out." Richelle snorted.

Kyle clicked back into autopilot. He dropped the hair from his hands, slid his underwear back on and walked past Richelle to the door. He looked through the peephole and saw a very large muscular woman he didn't recognize on the other side. Her pale head was topped with jet black dreadlocks that ran past her shoulders. She was wearing a necklace with a small skull on it that appeared to have been carved out of an actual skull.

"Who are you?" Kyle asked through the intercom.

"Is there a Kyle Soliano there?" The woman asked. A glint from the grill on her teeth flashed across the fish eye lens.

Kyle glanced back at the locked door to his office as he scratched his legs. His survival instincts screamed for him to get a very large gun right now, but Richelle was still in his apartment.

"Who wants to know?" Kyle replied as he scratched at the top of his chest.

A second woman burst through the wall to the left side of his doorway, leaving a hole that reached from floor to ceiling. A forest of long blonde dreadlocks shot out from the top of her head and nearly rubbed against Kyle's ceiling. Bits of what used to be Kyle's wall got caught on the various skull shaped pins that adorned her blue leather jacket.

She flashed Kyle a chrome toothed grin and it appeared that she had sharpened two of her teeth into fangs.

Maxine had long ago chosen the werewolf as her spirit animal. When another assassin made this the butt of a joke during a company meeting, Maxine spent the following night furiously sharpening her teeth into fangs. The next day she tore out the man's jugular with her teeth, disposed of his head in the compost bin and stole his chair.

"We're here to crush your head." Spoke the musclebound hulk in an unsettlingly deep yet polite tone. She punched Kyle right in the gut and sent him flying backwards down the hall towards his kitchen. These two were definitely taking some good drugs.

Kyle gasped for breath as he grabbed his chest. His ribs felt like they were on fire but he didn't feel any fractures. His newfound layer of fat had provided some cushioning. What little painkillers were still in his system managed to keep the pain from overwhelming him.

Richelle screamed and ran to far the corner of Kyle's bedroom as the smaller woman entered through the hole in the wall.

"Hey Enyo, is she on the list?" The giant blonde woman pointed back at Richelle with her thumb.

"Let me see." The shorter pale woman thumbed through her phone. "No, see Maxine, she's not on the posting. Leave her." She tucked her phone back into her pocket and the two of them headed for Kyle.

He scrambled to his feet and grabbed the silencer with hollow point bullets that he kept behind his fridge. The slide snapped a round into the chamber just as the large blonde woman came around the corner.

He fired a shot point blank into the forehead of the woman. The bullet failed to penetrate and instead just scraped some skin off, revealing the chrome sheen of metal beneath it.

They weren't wearing grills on their teeth; all of the bones in their bodies had been printed with a metal coating. Swapping one of the cell cartridges in a bioprinter for titanium or other alloys allowed for armor plated bones, preventatively reinforced knees, built-in brass knuckles and nipples with rings pre-installed.

As with many professional assassins, Kyle had tried metalizing his body parts at one point and he was not a fan of it. Having to be extra careful around metal detectors was bad enough, but having to remember to pop in a metallic suppository every day to replenish the metal that his body purged out of his system got old fast.

"Shit." Kyle said with a quiver in his voice. He lowered the barrel of his gun to take aim at her left eye. There wouldn't be any metal there to block a bullet getting to her brain. Before he could get a shot off she clamped her thick and heavy hand around his gun barrel. Kyle could see the printed in steel knuckles protruding from the back of her hand. She ripped the slide off his gun and smiled at him as she tossed it behind her.

He threw a punch at her abdomen and his hand recoiled in pain. It was like punching the wall of a building.

Maxine threw a punch at Kyle. He dodged it and took a

shot at her neck. It was softer there but he still couldn't cause any damage. She recovered and tried to bring her fist down on Kyle's outstretched arm. He deflected the blow and leaned all of his body weight on her arm to drive it into the drain of his sink. With a precise flex of his right butt cheek Kyle hit the switch for the garbage disposal.

Although the blades only managed to go around twice before they jammed on the metal bones, they ground through the flesh and into Maxine's arm enough to pin her in place.

Not one to waste an opportunity, Kyle yanked his wok down from the rack hanging over his sink and slammed it into Maxine's face with a satisfying clang of metal on metal violence.

"Do you smell what my wok is cooking!" Kyle yelled as he got two more hits in on the woman's head with the wok. She punched into the wok as Kyle swung it at her a third time. Her metal knuckles put a major fist shaped dent into the middle of it. She then ripped the wok from Kyle's grip and snarled at him with her fangs bared.

Enyo went around Maxine to get within arm's reach of Kyle. He leapt over his counter and dove for the bottom of his couch. He slid along the tiled floor and reached underneath to grab the shotgun with explosive rounds that he had hidden inside of it.

He punched into the hardwood false bottom. The wood didn't budge, pain burned through his knuckles and his hand fell back down to the cold floor.

Enyo rushed over and stomped on the back of his left

leg. The bones snapped and the muscles flattened as she drove her foot through the floor of his living room.

Kyle cried out as he felt the most intense pain he had felt in two decades. Trace amounts of painkillers tried to keep the pain at bay but they only gave him moments of control. His breathing sped up and sweat broke out all over his body. He rolled over in agony and saw Enyo standing over him.

"Who sent you?" Kyle managed to squeak out as he shivered on the floor. His heart slammed into the bruise on his chest with every quick beat, hurting from the inside.

"None of your business. You know that."

Enyo raised her other foot and brought it over Kyle's head. They were serious about that head crushing thing. Kyle stared at the pattern on the bottom of her boot as it blocked out the rest of the world around him.

Three armor piercing bullets clinked off the inside of Enyo's forehead and left metal dents protruding from her skin. Blood ran down from her nose as she crumpled over to the side. Her metal teeth pinged off of the tile as she hit the floor with a thud.

Kyle's eyes widened and a large smile fought its way past the pain shooting through him. Kira stood at the end of the hallway in her full motorcycle armor with a smoking silenced machine pistol in one hand and her black helmet with a copper visor in the other. She slid an orange messenger bag off her shoulders and let it slump gently to the floor.

"Enyo!" Maxine roared as she tore the garbage disposal

out of Kyle's sink.

Kira slid around the corner and fired at Maxine's head.

Maxine blocked the shot with the garbage disposal. She swung the garbage disposal at Kira.

Kira blocked it with her helmet. She pushed back against Maxine with all of her might, but she couldn't move her. The giant blonde smiled a toothy grin as she snarled down at Kira.

"My, what nice teeth you have." Kira said as she dropped her gun. She grabbed Maxine's jaw and kicked her square in the chest, tearing her jaw out.

Blood erupted from the gaping wound in Maxine's face where her jaw had been. Gurgled screams filled the apartment. Kira looked down over her and jammed the two prongs on the backend of the metal jawbone through Maxine's eyes. The screaming intensified. At last Kira brought her helmet down and hammered the jawbone deep into Maxine's brain. A loud metal on metal clang echoed through the apartment.

Then there was silence.

Kira let out a sigh of relief and set her bloody helmet on Kyle's kitchen counter. She pulled out her phone and took a picture of the slain assassin.

#jawpwned

A sound came from Kyle's bedroom. Kira snatched up her gun and wheeled around to face it. Richelle slowly walked out of the bedroom with her hands up.

"You with them?" Kira asked as her gun tracked Richelle's forehead.

"No. No, I just need to get out of here." Richelle pleaded. "Can you please let me go?"

"It's ok, she's with me!" Kyle shouted as he squirmed across the floor of his living room.

Kira examined Richelle's clothes and rolled her eyes. "Get out of here." Richelle bolted out of the hole in the wall. Kira picked up her messenger bag and walked back over to Kyle.

"Thank you!" Kyle gasped out as he fought to catch his breath. "How did you know those two were here?"

"I didn't. I figured you could use a mimosa or three to cushion the blow of getting fired." She held up her messenger bag and pulled out a bottle of champagne and a bottle of orange juice and set them on the counter. "Looks like you already found your own way of getting over things though."

"Thanks."

Kira picked Kyle up off of the floor and set him down on his couch. She examined the wound to his leg. One of Kyle's leg bones was poking out of his skin and the other was surrounded by a growing dark purple bulge. She pulled out a bio-seal patch from her bag and placed it over the wound. The adhesive gel stopped the bleeding and the local anesthetic numbed the area so Kyle wouldn't feel any pain for a few hours.

"Looks like you've had enough fun for one morning already. How about I help get you to the hospital and we can do the mimosas after we get back?"

"That would be excellent." Kyle said as the painkillers in the patch started to take effect.

"Any idea who these two were?" Kira asked as she took a picture of the dented forehead of the assassin she had shot for her portfolio.

#poppedlikeazit

"No idea. They said something about a posting." He scooted to the far side of his couch and reached over the edge and into Enyo's pockets. He fished out her cellphone and pulled one of her eyelids open to unlock it with the retina scanner. "Let's take a look."

The Hitboard app was already running on the phone. A red heart indicator was also flashing on the top of the screen, probably just a fitness tracker that was searching for a signal. Kyle opened up the Active Jobs list and found a Hitboard posting for him.

"Oh, shit. Someone put a hit out on me." Kyle gasped out.

"Well, you are a freelancer now. No company protection anymore." Kira replied as she came behind the couch and looked over his shoulder. "Who posted it?"

"Let me see." Kyle scrolled down for the link to the poster's profile page. Before he could click on the link, the flashing heart icon disappeared and the phone exploded, blowing his right hand off at the wrist. "You have got to be fucking kidding me!"

CHAPTER SIX

Kyle hopped into to the lobby of the Advanced Performance Health hospital. The scenery in the lobby hadn't changed much since the day before, but there was a different nurse waiting at the reception desk. Kyle tightened the grip of his left arm around Kira's shoulders for support as he moved. The toes of his crushed leg brushed along the floor as the two of them awkwardly moved forward.

"This would be a lot easier if I just carried you." Kira said as she pulled him back upright. She had helped him put some shorts on so he wouldn't have to be dragged around in his underwear. Putting on pants over a crushed leg was out of the question.

"Like a newlywed bride? No way." Kyle huffed back. "Come on, the receptionist is right there. We can do this." Kyle gestured toward the desk with his sealing patch covered stump.

The nurse at the reception desk let out several increasingly long sighs as she watched the pair of them shamble towards her.

"Hello. Can I help you?" The nurse asked.

"Yes. I need a new hand and a new leg." Kyle waved his stump and shook his hip to flail his crushed leg around. "Can you take me in now? My cells should still be on file."

"Great." The nurse responded dryly. "Yes, we should be able to help. Have you been here before?"

"Yeah, I was here yesterday. I got some new legs and an arm."

"You already lost them?"

"Not all of them." Kyle hopped on his good leg. "See, this one's still good and this is the new arm. I lost the old one. What does it matter? I lead an exciting life." He pushed his good thumb into the scanner. "I'm covered for all this, trust me. Can you make sure they tan everything to match this time? I'm not a fan of this whole white gloves look."

"You certainly appear to be a frequent customer." The nurse said as she looked over his file. "Sir, it appears that you have had your coverage reduced since the last time you were here. You are currently limited to one limb replacement every six months. Would you like us to print you a new leg or a new hand?"

"What? You mean I have to choose?" Kyle tried to lean forward but started to lose his grip and pulled himself back up to Kira's shoulder. "Can't we just do both now and charge the second one in six months or something?"

"No, sir. I'm afraid I can't do that."

"Well, can I just pay you to do the extra limb now? I

have money."

"I'm sorry sir, we can't accept cash payment. We have to go through your insurance, it's a billing issue."

"It's a billing issue that you don't want to get paid for things?" Kyle raised an eyebrow at the nurse.

"Sir, you are holding up the line. Which is it going to be?" The nurse straightened her back and stared Kyle down.

He looked over his shoulder, there was no line.

"What do you think?" Kyle asked Kira.

"Get the leg. At least then I won't have to carry your sorry ass around." She readjusted her grip on him.

"Ok, I'll do the leg." He made a sloppy signature on the tablet with his left hand and the nurse called a wheelchair for him.

*****

Two hours later Kyle walked back into the lobby on his new leg. Kira was sitting in a chair halfway through drinking a smoothie, looking at her phone. He slumped down into the chair next to her.

"Did they tan it to match?" Kira tucked her phone back into her pocket.

"No." Kyle grimaced. He held up his left leg which now had three different color bands of skin on it. Dark skin on his thigh abruptly changed to pale skin around his knee, which then became even paler around his calf. "This sucks."

"Well, at least you only have to wait six months to get that stump replaced." Kira smiled as she held up her hand to fist bump him. Kyle stump bumped her back and shook his head in disgust. "How about we swing back by my place on the way back so you can pick up your rifle? It looks like you're going to have to deal with people at long range for the time being."

"That old thing? No way. I'm not going to be like this for long."

"You sure?" Kira gestured towards the stump on his arm.

"Yeah." Kyle nodded. "You can toss that piece of junk for all I care."

"Fine, whatever you say." Kira rolled her eyes and took a big sip of her smoothie. "Oh, by the way. Your phone has been making sizzling noises for the past hour." Kira handed Kyle his phone.

Kyle unlocked his phone and took a look at his messages. His eyes perked open and he straightened his back. A faint smile returned to his face.

"A headhunter contacted me." He said as he looked over the e-mail on his phone.

"What? Another assassin?" Kira replied as her eyes started scanning the people in the lobby.

"No, the other kind." He rapidly scrolled up and down through the message. "He must have seen on Hitboard that I got laid off. This guy says that he wants to setup an interview for me with Crafts of Khartoum, today."

"Oooh, that's Nadima Qosi's team." Kira peered over at the message on Kyle's phone. "The Sudanese Serpent herself. She would be great for you to work with. Her outfit specializes in poisons, you could learn a lot on how to be sneaky from them."

"It says that the opening is immediate and they want to meet today. Crap, how am I supposed to get a job without a hand?"

"I'm sure it'll be fine. She knows the business and besides, if she hires you you'll get a new one anyway. Go for it."

*****

Kyle arrived at the entrance to Crafts of Khartoum late in the afternoon. The luxury furniture store was located on the ground floor of a small apartment building next to a gas station. The front door was locked shut and a sign saying 'By Appointment Only' was etched in to a gold panel above the intercom.

He pushed the buzzer on the intercom.

"Hello, do you have an appointment?" A camera above the entrance swiveled around to examine him.

"Yes, I'm here for the interview." He waved to the camera with his left hand and kept his stump buried in his business suit pocket. Kyle didn't have time to buy a new suit before the interview. His new flab pushed against the seams of the suit with every move he made. The silenced pistol and knives in his pockets bulged out noticeably from underneath the tight fitting suit. Whoever was on security here wouldn't need any ultrasonic or radar scans to tell he was armed.

"One moment." Gears inside the doors clanged against each other. "Please step inside and place all weapons into the drawer."

Kyle stepped inside the vestibule. The outer doors closed behind him and left him in a clear plastic box with no air holes. He gently placed his silencer, extra clip and throwing knives into the drawer in front of him and it slid shut. Kyle breathed a little easier as the emptied pockets gave his stomach more room to flow into. The top of the box opened up and the barrel of a minigun looked down on him. Kyle looked down and saw a drain built into the floor below him. This place did not tolerate messes.

A retinal scanner slid up to the front of the box and scanned his eyes. The retinal scanner retracted and a radar array spun around the box to scan for any other weapons. At last, a green light flashed and a tall woman in a metallic emerald pantsuit walked up to the door of the box.

"Hello, Kyle, so nice to finally meet you." Nadima said as she opened up the security door using a keypad on the other side. "I'm Nadima Qosi, owner of Crafts of Khartoum." She held out her hand as he stepped out into the office. Her long silky hair draped over one shoulder and had gold rings at the ends. A faint hexagon texture gleamed from the emerald surface of her suit in the light.

"Nice to meet you too. Kyle reached out with his left hand, keeping his stump firmly jammed into his pocket.

"Ah, a right brained person. We don't get many like you here." Nadima switched hands to shake Kyle's left. "You seem smaller than you look in the pictures."

"Oh, you know how it is. Just the pills wearing off. Not a problem though, it's all mental really in this line of work."

"Indeed it is. Please come this way." Nadima gestured towards the back end of the gallery with her hand. Several golden dots on the bottoms of her fingers matched the gold nail polish on the other side.

Gold plating was typically used on chemical sensors due to the high corrosion resistance. As a specialist in poisons and other potentially fatal chemicals, Nadima had installed several such sensors into her fingertips. These could give her an analysis of anything she touched in her eyes only display or they could be wired directly into her taste buds.

Had she just tasted him? Kyle shook the thought out of his mind and focused back on the interview.

"Nice setup you have here." Kyle said as he examined the office. Various fancy looking couches and chairs made out of stained wood and leather were scattered in the gallery on the other side of the security door. Absurdly high prices painted on to canvas tags adorned each piece of furniture.

"Thank you. Our old place in Khartoum was setup like an antiques shop to try and blend in, but we kept getting tourists. At least, they claimed to be tourists." She paused by several large tanks of chemicals sitting next to a workbench with a bunch of tools and lab equipment on top of it. The tools and equipment were all in pristine condition and the tanks were not all full. "Fortunately for us, it turns out that many chemicals used to treat wood and fabric can be quite poisonous to humans in the correct proportions." She turned around and smiled back at Kyle.

"Oh yes, that's very convenient." Kyle nodded in approval. Nadima searched his face then narrowed her eyes and continued walking towards her office.

"Would you like any coffee or something else to drink?" Nadima sat down in her puffy executive leather chair and turned her screen so only she could see it.

"Coffee would be great." Kyle said as he sat down in a much stiffer chair directly in front of her. He resisted the urge to put his right arm on the arm rest and instead wedged his right arm against the corner of the chair to keep the stump in his pocket.

"Whitney, can you please bring us two coffees? Thank you." Nadima said into her headset. She glanced once more at her screen and then turned to Kyle. "Thank you again for coming in on such short notice. We recently lost an operative in the field and we were so happy that Darren was able to find someone with experience in this line of work so quickly. I've barely even had time to look over your resume."

"Not a problem. Thank you for the opportunity." Kyle kept his back straight in the chair. "May I ask what happened to your last employee?"

"She was out on an assignment in Europe. Managed to place the poison on the dinner of the target but she got caught on her way out after he died. I believe they dunked her in acid from what I have been able to find out."

"Ouch, that sucks." Kyle nodded.

The advent of bioprinting meant that it was no longer profitable to sell organs from captives that might be rejected by the recipient so there was no reason to keep the bodies of captured assassins intact. It made burial services in the assassin community increasingly rare. "Well, I'm sure I'll be able to not only fill in for her, but give you even more bang for your buck."

"I see." Nadima continued looking over his resume. "As you can probably tell, we typically focus on poisons and other chemical methods for taking down our targets. I don't see anything like that here on your résumé. Have you had any recent experience with poisons, allergic reactions or anything like that?"

"Lately I've been dealing more with explosives, but planting a poison isn't too different from planting a bomb." Kyle responded as he waved his hand around. A cold sweat broke out on the back of his neck. "I do have a lot of experience escaping capture though, so what happened to your previous agent will not be a problem for me." Kyle smiled a wide grin. "In fact I was captured on my last assignment." Nadima's eyes went wide and she looked sternly at him. Kyle paused for a moment to search for the most positive sounding words he could use. "Thankfully, I was able to use all of my experience to overcome that difficulty, escape and take out the target. It's right there on my profile. See for yourself."

"Yes, I see that you stabbed him in the eye with a piece of a helicopter blade?"

"Yes, well, technically I fired a grenade at the helicopter. Then the helicopter blade snapped and stabbed him. But, I was the reason all of that happened." He replied with a confident grin.

Whitney, Nadima's secretary entered the office with two steaming cups of coffee. The mug was almost to Kyle's lips when he noticed that Nadima was stirring hers around with one of her sensor studded fingers. Was this just a nervous habit or was her secretary trying to kill her?

He lowered his mug back down to his leg and waited for Nadima to take a sip first.

"You went after your target with a grenade launcher? Those are pretty loud. Didn't his men chase after you?" Nadima leaned over her desk towards Kyle. She took a sip of her coffee and gave him a concerned look.

"Well, by that time I had already gunned down most of them." Kyle took a deep sip of coffee. "Or they had been blown up when I turned their kitchen into a pipe bomb. You see, I'm very resourceful and I can improvise whenever I need to get out of a bad situation. Sometimes the goons find you when you are trying to poison someone, if they find me, they're dead too."

"Interesting approach. Why did Vitron lay you off? You clearly have a talent for making something from nothing."

"Thank you." Kyle nodded vigorously in response. "It's

a silly reason really. They said I was losing too many limbs and other parts while I was working. My clients were all very happy with the results though as you can see."

"Yes, I believe I do." Nadima looked down at her coffee and took another sip. She picked up a pen from her desk and threw it at Kyle's right side.

Kyle yanked the stump out of his pocket to catch the pen. It bounced off the end of his stump. Kyle's eyes bulged out as he glanced back and forth between the stump and Nadima's searing gaze.

"I was wondering why you were hiding that hand. I thought you were hiding a weapon, but it looks like you are just hiding shame. Was that left over from the Caribbean?"

"No." Kyle let out an exasperated breath. "This is from yesterday." He took another breath to regain some composure. "It won't matter though, once I'm back on a new health plan I'll be fully re-armed and back on the pills again, just like new!"

"Kyle," Nadima put her mug down on top of a thick leather cup holder. "I can pick any person off the street and pump them full of drugs and spare limbs to get them to do what your most recent experience shows. You can't even keep yourself together outside of work. I cater to a clientele that is much more concerned with subtlety than those mobsters Vitron had you working for. I need someone who can strike a target without having to blow up a whole building to do it."

"I get it. I get it. That's a great thing to strive for." Kyle looked down and swirled his coffee around a few times. "If

I could prove that I could do that, would you change your mind?"

"Perhaps. If you can pull off something restrained and clever before we find a new assassin, I may reconsider. For now though, thank you for your time. You can pick up your guns on the way out." Nadima's face went cold and she gestured with her head towards the door.

"Thank you for your consideration." He held out his stump to shake her hand. Nadima raised an eyebrow. Kyle smiled awkwardly as he pulled the stump back and offered his remaining hand.

CHAPTER SEVEN

Kyle stared down at the cup of coffee sitting on the table in front of him. He silently stirred the cream around with a stirrer. Air carrying the sweet smells of freshly grilled cheeseburgers circled around him.

"It's ok, you'll get other chances." Kira said with a smile. She sipped her coffee and checked over her shoulder. "Look on the bright side, you've only been unemployed for two days and you've already had an interview. That's a pretty good start." She titled her head down to get a look at his eyes.

"Yeah, I suppose." Kyle looked longingly at the Redline Burger menu behind him. This restaurant specialized in caffeinated meats for the energy craving meat lover. "Maybe I should get a cheeseburger to celebrate."

"No, Kyle, no cheeseburgers." Kira glared at the menu and turned back to him. "I should have known it was a bad idea meeting here."

"They're close to my place and they have very strong coffee." Kyle replied as he took a deep breath of the delicious aroma filling the restaurant. "They also make delicious meaty espresso filled things."

"That whole menu is full of temptation that your body can't get rid of anymore." Kira scolded him. "Right now you need to stay focused on the task at hand."

Kyle shot her a disapproving look and held up his stump.

"Oh yeah, sorry. Anyway, you just need to get a new hand and have some more interviews and I'm sure you'll find something."

"She said she couldn't trust me with any delicate situations." Kyle sighed as he leaned back into his seat.

"Well, you can prove her wrong. We get you a new hand, find an easy target and figure out some restrained and clever way for you to take them out without losing any more limbs. Easy. Right?"

"I don't think a new hand is going to be enough." Kyle looked down at his stump.

The corner of his eye caught a small child staring at him from the next table over. The kid covered one eye and shouted "Arrr!"

"Thank you. I am not a pirate." Kyle waved his stump to the kid. He turned back to Kira and let out a low growl of frustration. "Have you ever tried any of those generic pill sources?"

"Kyle." Kira put down her coffee and leaned in towards him. "Don't ever try any of those black market pills. Those things have to be customized to match your genes in order to work. I've seen what happens when people take them and it is not pretty. You don't want your body suddenly secreting blue liquid or changing colors in the sunlight or some other random weird ass side effect do you? Right?"

"Yeah, I guess."

"Good. You need to stick with the body you have and work from there. It'll take time and I know you hate having to be patient, but that's your only option right now. You can do it." She held up her coffee cup in front of him.

"Thanks Kira." The two of them tapped their coffee cups together.

*****

Kyle zipped up his jacket to block the wind. A cool breeze off the coast blew through his hair and pressed the loose fitting jacket against his body. He was standing in line to get into the Foam Lounge, an upscale bar in the Financial District. Perfectly dosed and manicured bodies surrounded him, huddled together for warmth. Kyle noticed the crowd but his eyes focused on the bar inside and the wonderful concoctions the bartenders here came up with. The drinks here always cheered him up.

Security consisted of a pair of bouncers who currently enjoyed the pills Kyle had not so long ago. After waiting for what felt like an hour in the cold, Kyle made his way to the front of the line. He presented his ID from his left pocket and lifted his arms for the pat down. The bouncer didn't feel any weapons as he worked his way up, but he felt something else on Kyle's stomach.

"Please open your jacket sir." The bouncer asked as he pointed a flashlight at Kyle's face.

"Uh, sure. Is there something wrong?" Kyle meekly asked as he pushed his stump into the jacket to hold it down while he unzipped it. The bouncer grabbed on to the flab of his stomach and shook his head.

"Sir, I'm afraid you can't come in here. We like to keep things classy here. There's a dive bar down the street, you can go there."

"Oh, come on!" Kyle pleaded. "I just want to grab a drink. That's it." He gestured towards the bar with the stump hiding inside his sleeve.

"Sir, I'm going to need you to show both hands!" The bouncer responded as he dropped back and his partner put his hand on something in his pocket.

"Fuck. It's just a stump, chill out." Kyle said as he pulled his sleeve down to reveal that he was partially unarmed.

"What are you supposed to be? Like a fat pirate or something?" The bouncer asked. The other bouncer and the guests in the line started laughing and elbowing Kyle out of the way.

"Why does everyone say pirate?" Kyle complained as he backed away. "Why not lumberjack or lion tamer or something else?"

"You can go be whatever you want down the street pal, just not here." The bouncer said as he body blocked Kyle from the door and nudged him towards the street with his butt.

*****

Pervasive itching all over his body woke him up several hours earlier than usual the following morning. He scrambled to the bathroom and doused himself with lavender oil to calm the thousands of angry hairs sprouting up all over him. His skin felt like Velcro when he ran a finger over his chest.

The fragrance of the lavender oil permeated the air underneath his bedsheets as he tried to go back to sleep. It was like trying to go to sleep inside of a shampoo bottle. Defeated, he pulled the covers off and got out of bed. He grabbed his phone and looked up the nearest gym. If he was going to have to be awake, he might as well do something useful.

The only gym for miles stood in front of Kyle in all its anachronistic glory. Seventy years ago, San Francisco had been practically overrun with competing, fancy up-scale gyms. Clean places with shiny new equipment and facilities that were attended by models, bankers, prostitutes and the lawyers who served them all.

Kyle stared at one of the few remaining ancient shrines to the purity of the human body. Despair and disgust mixed in his eyes as he gazed on the source of his impending doom.

Corroded concrete adorned the outside of the building, which had once been a bank. Every time the door opened the stench of sweat and cleaning agents polluted the nearby air and revealed the true contents now held within these walls. Kyle paused in front of the doorway as he tried to acclimate himself to a lighter degree of odor before he ventured inside. Two old hippies who would never corrupt their bodies with legal drugs walked out. Sweat dripped through shirts that must have been nearly as old as their owners as they walked past him. A pair of grad students who looked to be in their early twenties walked in. Perhaps when they were older they would be able to afford to look how commercials showed people in their twenties should look.

Kyle was about to become one of the damned.

"For the cheeseburgers." Kyle reminded himself. He clenched his fist and walked inside.

An old man with leathery skin and thick glasses stood behind the counter as Kyle entered. Not even something as useful as a freshly printed set of eyes was to be found in this time capsule. The old man gestured for Kyle to come forward with a forearm that was surprisingly muscular for a natural old hippie. Kyle signed up but turned down the offer for a discount for signing up for a whole year. He didn't plan on needing to come in for that long.

"Would you like a personal trainer?" The old man asked.

"Sure, I haven't been to one of these in a while. Who you got?" Kyle responded. The old man handed Kyle a notebook, filled with paper, showing the currently active personal trainers. Apparently the only computer in the place was the one he had just signed up on. As he flipped through the pages, one trainer in particular caught Kyle's eye. "I'll take Reuben. He's got a good name and I really like those sandwiches."

"That's a good pick. He'll do you right." The old hippie waved over a burly looking Filipino man who was talking to another trainer just behind the desk. Reuben approached wearing a sweat wicking red shirt that was one size too small. Reuben looked like he had access to the cheeseburger pills, but Kyle knew it was probably just because he spent every waking moment lifting things or telling other people to lift things. How monotonous. Reuben must have suffered brain damage from the fumes at this place and now lifting things seemed new to him every time.

Reuben went to shake Kyle's right hand and Kyle waved his stump at him.

"I guess no barbells today then, huh?" Reuben joked as he shook Kyle's left hand instead.

"Yeah, not today." Kyle agreed as he tried to remember what a barbell was.

Reuben opened up the door to the main part of the gym and the stench of sweat and cleaning agents intensified as Kyle walked ever deeper into the bowels of the building. No wonder the insurance companies could charge so much for drugs that let people avoid these places, he could already feel the stench of it permeating his skin.

Several monitors played cheesy training montages from a

century ago. Oily, tanned people demonstrated all of the equipment. Apparently, you needed someone yelling at you to get the full benefit of using it.

Reuben did not disappoint in this respect, though he was more of a nurturing gentler meathead that the ones in the videos. Kyle considered asking him to yell in an angrier voice to improve his workout, but decided to save that for when he had both hands.

Two hours, a dozen machines, several sets of free weights and one stability ball later, every part of Kyle's body felt like it was on fire. Reuben had even figured out how to strap a weight to the stump so Kyle could avoid something called 'bowler's arm', which was probably some kind of disease that thrived in environments like this.

He slumped on to a bench and took a sip of water from the cup Reuben handed him. Kyle looked down. The gut was still there, taunting him.

"Well, that was pointless." Kyle sighed as he finished the water in the cup.

"It will take a few weeks before you start to see much of an improvement. But the hardest part is over. You're past your first day." Reuben put his hand up for a high five. Summoning all his remaining energy, Kyle met him up high with his two tone arm.

"So, same thing tomorrow?" Kyle asked, still breathing heavily.

"Don't try to lift every day or your muscles won't get the rest they need to grow stronger."

"Crap, this is going to take twice as long?" Kyle said in

an exasperated voice.

"We'll hit the pool tomorrow." Reuben said as he slapped Kyle on the shoulder.

"Thanks, I think I'll use the pool in my building." Kyle had seen the pool here during the tour and had decided any swimming would be done on the roof deck of his chic apartment building instead. He was training to fight assassins, not infection.

Kyle slowly walked out of the gym. It took all of his effort just to keep moving so his burning muscles wouldn't lock up on him. A blast of cool air made all of the tiny hairs on his body stand on end, but he was too tired to scratch at them. Across the street from the gym was a burger joint, one of the Grubburger franchises. They were not nearly as delicious as Kokumi, but they were much greasier.

Through the windows of the restaurant Kyle could see all the people inside enjoying the greasy cheese covered delight that the drugs flowing through their bodies would metabolize into more muscle, rendering their burgers guilt free. Kyle looked down at his sweat covered stump. This was not how things were going to be for the next six months.

CHAPTER EIGHT

Kyle awoke several hours later in a hospital bed. The top of the bed had been raised and the memory foam in the pillow gently supported his head. He looked down and saw his new right hand resting on top of the bed sheet. He moved his fingers and felt the texture of the sheets. They weren't as smooth as the luxury sheets that his old hospital had, but he wasn't here for the bedding.

Frustrated with the six months he would have to wait to get a new hand on his COBRA plan, Kyle had looked up the following on his way back from the gym:

'HEALTH INSURANCE NEW HAND NOW'

The first hit to show up near him was an HMO called Charity Health that advertised same day limb replacements if you signed up before noon. Kyle beat the cutoff by twenty minutes.

"Mr. Soliano, so sorry for the delay. How does the hand feel?" Dr. Gallo asked. He glanced back and forth between Kyle's hand and his tablet.

"Good." Kyle tapped his new fingers to his thumb and

palm. Charity Health was good but they still relied on manual testing instead of automated shocks to see if limbs were working. "Well worth the wait."

This had been Kyle's first time at a Charity Health hospital so they had needed to grow fresh cells in a rapid incubator to fill up the bioprinter cartridges. Kyle wondered what his old insurer had done with the leftover cell cartridges at his previous hospital.

Kyle's previous hospital was decidedly high end, and they disposed of unwanted leftover cell cartridges by incinerating the entire cartridge. More budget conscious hospitals simply sterilized the cartridges and then refilled them with another patient's cells, a process that legally allowed for up to five percent of the cells in a given cartridge to be from people who were not the current patient. Other hospitals simply tossed them into the trash, where they would eventually begin leaking and mix with other people's genetic information in a garbage dump full of discarded cell cartridges. This was also the basis for a bad horror movie that Kyle had seen the year before.

"Due to the limits with your current plan we didn't pre-tan your hand to match." Dr. Gallo continued. "Is that ok or would you like to pay to have it tanned?"

"That's fine." Kyle responded. The premiums for this HMO were already three times what his previous plan cost. His bank account could only withstand this company for eight months. "It's not like the rest of me matches either."

"Yes, we noticed that. Was that work done here? We didn't see anything about other limbs on your records."

"No, that was at my old company the past two days." Kyle said from behind a screen as he put his clothes back on. "Say, can you write me a prescription for those cheeseburger pills while you're here?"

"I'm sorry, cheeseburger pills? Do you mean the enzyme pills that convert fat into muscle?"

"Yeah, those. How much extra for those?"

"I'm sorry, we don't cover those here."

"Dammit." Kyle cursed under his breath. "Fine. I'll figure something else out."

"Very well, everything looks to be in order. Since you are new here I will email you a link to our phone app that you can use if you need anything else."

Kyle hopped into the back seat of a cab and immediately put his new fingers to work looking up black market pills on the internet with his phone. Pharmaceutical Imports from Canada appeared and Kyle clicked on the link. If it came from Canada it wasn't really black market then was it?

After a few minutes of searching through the site he found a way to order drugs for delivery to the US for 'educational purposes only'. The price was still significantly higher than he expected, but he only needed enough to last him until he got a new job. A single dose of either the fat converting enzyme pills or the hair removal pills would cost him a month's mortgage. The lavender oil was doing a pretty good job to control the itching so the hair removal pills could wait. Kyle placed an order for the generic muscle enzyme pills, rush delivery. The pills were due to arrive by noon the next day.

Kyle relaxed deep into the bench seat at back of the cab. Everything was going to be ok.

*****

Reuben rudely awoke Kyle the following morning when he called to see where he was. Kyle had canceled his appointments for the week; he wouldn't need them once the delivery arrived. He slathered himself in lavender oil and went back to sleep. The scent of lavender had started to take permanent hold of the airspace in his bedroom.

Just after 10am the drone dock started chiming, his drugs had arrived. Kyle leapt out of bed and made a beeline to his kitchen. The motors were still whirring as the landing bay retracted into the apartment. Kyle eagerly stood right next to the hatch as he waited for the door to unlock. With a swift motion of his new hand, Kyle flipped open the hatch and swiped out the delivery.

The pills were wrapped haphazardly in multiple layers of white paper and packing tape. A piece of paper stating '100% AUTHANTIC' fell out of the package after Kyle chopped the end off with his trusty kitchen cleaver. He tore through the inner packaging and found the vial with the pills in it. They were the same green color as the pills he used to take. That was a good sign.

Anxiously, Kyle unscrewed the lid on the container and picked two pills out of it. He rolled them around in his palm and examined them for any defects. The looked like the same green pills as before. There were no bulges or cuts or leaks anywhere that he could see. They even felt the same weight.

He pulled the rest of the packaging out. Aside from the piece of paper declaring these pills '100% AUTHANTIC', there wasn't any of the usual warnings or instructions that typically came with drugs. Kyle looked down at the pills again. What was the worst that could happen? Kira had mentioned blue pee and changing skin color, but any side effects would just be temporary. Hell, randomly changing skin color might even be kind of fun. It would certainly get him into more bars.

Kyle popped the pills in his mouth and swallowed.

CHAPTER NINE

Kyle stepped into the Redline Burger restaurant. They weren't the best burger in town but before eleven they were the closest open option. He could still see, hear and taste after taking the pills, so at least they weren't immediately poisonous. His body hadn't changed at all though. Maybe the drugs just needed some protein and fat to work with? That theory served as good an excuse as any for a cheeseburger.

The breakfast rush was over, so he faced no crowds as he headed up to the register and contemplated which of the caffeinated meats he wanted to test his new drugs with. A little extra caffeine might even jump start the reaction. He ordered a Black Eye Burger and grabbed a seat at the coffee bar. The two shots of espresso mixed into the patty would be perfect to help get his old body back as fast as possible.

There were only a few patrons in the restaurant. Over his shoulder Kyle saw a man in a hoodie sipping coffee with a half-eaten breakfast sandwich while he typed away on a very large metal framed laptop. A pair of women chatted about something dirty as they shared a tray of coffee ground crusted bacon in a booth further down. Two more people ate early lunches alone at the tables by the opposite wall. He had the whole bar to himself.

"Can I get you anything?" The bearded barista asked him.

"I got a Black Eye coming, but can you get me a mocha too?" Kyle responded. More caffeine in his system would only speed up the effects of the pills and that could only be a good thing.

The mocha showed up just before Kyle's burger did. His heart rate increased from the contact high as he breathed in air infused with caffeine. The banquet of flavors from the burger permeated the air in front of his face, and he took a deep breath to savor the moment. A dreadful future without cheeseburgers ended here. Hints of espresso and cheese tickled his tongue as Kyle pulled the scented air down into to his lungs. His body tensed in anticipation of the transformation that was about to occur.

Kyle took a small bite out of the cheeseburger. He paused for a minute and poked his biceps and stomach. Nothing had changed, but it was only the first bite. He took a few more cautious bites, pausing each time to poke his stomach and arms.

He let out a sigh and shook his head. Nearly a third of the burger was gone and still no effect. The burger on his plate stared at him defiantly. Kyle stared back angrily. He had just wasted a ton of cash on useless pills, but that was no reason to leave a good cheeseburger unfinished.

Kyle seized the burger and chomped into it. Just as he was about to go for another bite, he felt something in his left arm. It was a tingling sensation. He poked his bicep and the tingling continued. Then his right bicep started to tingle too. In mere seconds he felt a rush of rejuvenation work its way through all the muscles in his body.

The pills were working!

Kyle devoured the rest of the cheeseburger and chugged his mocha. His entire body felt like it was being massaged with a thousand tiny cattle prods. These pills worked fast. He might just walk out of this restaurant completely fit. The only Reubens he would see from now on would be edible.

The power of the shocks inside of him intensified. Kyle spun around on his barstool and smiled. Such a strong effect must be obliterating the fat inside his body.

The tingling increased and his body started to shiver all over.

His foot slammed into the counter without so much as denting the plywood. Then Kyle's other leg spasmed upwards and drove his knee into the edge of the bar. Kyle grabbed his leg in pain, then one arm shot out to the side. He had to clench his teeth to keep from screaming out in pain.

His ab muscles contracted and pulled his face into the empty plate in front of him. Bits of grease and cheese smeared over his face as he fought to pull himself back up.

Multiple spasms around his neck jerked his head in every direction. He tried to call for help but the muscles in his jaw tightened and he couldn't open his mouth.

Unable to speak or scream Kyle snorted and growled as he fought to regain control of his body. The other customers in the restaurant shot him odd glances as he slammed his right fist uncontrollably into the top of the counter. His left arm knocked a napkin dispenser off the bar.

Sweat formed on Kyle's increasingly red face as he struggled with a body gone haywire. Would he need a cab to get home? Could he even use his phone well enough to call a cab in this condition?

As he struggled to keep his head facing forward, a small red headed woman sat down on the bar stool next to him. She sipped on a latte while she watched Kyle twitch.

"Hi there." The woman said. "How's it going?"

"Hi! I'm Kyle." He spat out quickly before his jaw had another chance to clamp shut. He was surprised that anyone would want to talk to him in this condition.

"I'm Mildred. I've seen you here around town a lot. I guess you could say I've been stalking you." Mildred said with the same giggle she had probably used when talking to boys in high school.

"You've been stalking me?" Kyle considered this for a second and made his decision. "That's kind of hot." His nose and ears twitched wildly in every direction.

His other knee jerked into the wall of the counter and he grimaced in pain. Mildred, a skinny, pale, redhead wearing red-rimmed glasses and a knee-length green coat, didn't seem at all concerned by this. Kyle wasn't typically a fan of the librarian look, but there was something in her eyes that suggested she was exciting underneath her studious exterior.

"I want to fucking rip you apart and light you on fire." Mildred said in a hushed voice so the rest of the restaurant wouldn't hear her.

"That's kinky." Kyle forced out as he tried to pull his an outstretched arm back in. He appreciated women who lacked subtlety. The bearded barista rolled his eyes and walked towards the other end of the bar. "What do you say you strike this match and get this fire started?"

"Oh, things are about to get very fiery here indeed." Mildred said as she put her head on her hands and looked into Kyle's eyes.

"What, you want to start making out here?" Kyle considered whether or not that might involve him accidentally head butting her. "Sweet. I'm down." He tried to lean in towards her but his back muscles spasmed and his shoulders pulled back like he was caught in invisible restraints.

Mildred continued to smile at him. She was definitely a weird one.

"Oh, no no no. Tell me Kyle, have you ever heard of Precision Blasting Incorporated? We're a competitor of your former employer." Mildred savored the words. "You may have heard of me, Mildred the Bomb Queen."

"Oh, fuck." Kyle said as the smile vanished from his

face, and he tried to lean away from her, despite his right elbow fighting him to get closer.

"Oh fuck indeed." Mildred continued. "Do you remember your trip to Burkina Faso a few years ago, when you assassinated the prince?"

"Umm, yeah, I remember the beard. It was so thick bullets left holes in it. His facial hair looked like Swiss cheese after I shot him. I always thought that was neat, I didn't know that could happen."

"And do you remember that you killed him by bursting into a room and mowing down everyone in it with a machine gun!" Mildred growled back. "Not exactly precise of you! And do you happen to remember an awkward looking person near the back that you killed along with everyone else in that room?"

"Umm, no? But then I guess everyone looks awkward when they're being shot at." Kyle replied. His entire body started to clench up. If he had to fight this woman he would be lucky to manage falling on her.

"No you asshole! He always looked awkward!" Mildred slammed her hand on the counter. "One of our people was there too, with a precisely rigged champagne flute loaded with a charge that would send a huge shard of glass straight into the brain of the prince and leave everyone else freaked out but otherwise alive. But no! You killed him before he could deliver it! His name was Gustav and I loved him and now I am going to send you to hell in the most painfully precise way ever!"

Kyle tried to stand up but his thigh muscles objected and

his butt remained clamped against the bar stool.

"Wait. Don't get up. Not yet." Mildred put her hand up. "I rigged your bar stool with an explosive while you were busy making a pig of yourself with your burger. It's a nice close range circumferential device. It was Gustav's favorite." She paused for a moment to swoon over her dearly departed Gustav. "I'd recommend you keep your ass glued to that seat, otherwise it will cut your legs off."

The explosive Mildred referred to was a close range anti-personnel mine. This particular variety contained a small shaped charge that was connected to a spiral of primacord wrapped inside of a bundle of razor wire. When triggered the explosive force would cause the razor wire to violently expand outward into a small circle and spin at several thousand rpm, cutting through any flesh that happened to be in the small radius of effect like a band saw. Mildred had positioned her chair so that the whirling ring of death would stop just a few inches short of her.

Kyle tried to relax back into the bar stool. The muscles in his left butt check started to twitch in suicidal fashion. He scoured the counter to see what weapons were available. On the counter within arm's reach of him were a napkin dispenser, a salt shaker, a spoon and a fork. All were valid options for weapons. Whether or not he could keep a grip on any of them long enough to use them as a weapon was another matter entirely.

"That's better. I want to savor this." Mildred licked her lips. "When I saw that ninja's Hitboard posting for you I couldn't resist."

"Wait. What ninja?" Kyle had killed or maimed many ninjas in his career. He needed her to be more specific. "Who put the hit out on me?" He pushed his right arm on the counter with his other arm, his hand close to the napkin dispenser.

"I have no idea who he is. All I know is that you are going to pay for what you did in Burkina Faso. I'm guessing that since you're a total asshole, you probably pissed him off in a similar fashion at some point."

Kyle thought back to the Burkina Faso assignment to see if he could remember any other assassins in the room. He hadn't really paid any attention to the rest of the people there since he had been focusing on the prince. Kyle had been the one to take that assignment. He should have been the only assassin there.

"Now wait a minute. I took the job off Hitboard fair and square. Why was your boyfriend even there?" Kyle's arm convulsed and his hand moved closer to the spoon.

"We were going to steal your kill. Our company is small, we kept getting outbid and we needed to make a name for ourselves."

"So your idiot boyfriend broke the rules and took a bullet for his trouble. Tough shit." Kyle's head started to shake back and forth but he locked eyes with Mildred to make sure she didn't look anywhere else. With a push from his other arm, he slowly moved his hand until the tips of his fingers touched the fork on the counter. "Crap like that is exactly what the bids are supposed to prevent. There's a reason for the rules, and it's not just to prevent the admins from sending a hit squad of ninjas after you in the middle of the night. If your shitty company can't follow the rules you'll have bigger problems than me. Let me guess, you and your boyfriend were a two person company?"

"He was my fiancé!" Mildred yelled at him as she hit her fist against the countertop. Kyle grabbed the fork off the counter and slammed it into the top of her hand as hard as he could. The fork met little resistance and went all the way through into the wooden countertop.

Mildred screamed. She was just a stock human.

"Oooo, I've got a pressure sensitive bomb. Oooo, I'm sooo badass." Kyle stuck out his tongue at Mildred and quickly reeled it back in in case his jaw locked up again. He pulled his unwilling leg up to the seat of the barstool so he was crouching on it. "Next time you should use a remote and not sit so close." Kyle leaned towards the bar and lurched his uncooperative body over the countertop.

Kyle covered his head with his hands and waited for the explosion and inevitable screaming that would follow.

Nothing happened.

A grenade landed in front of Kyle. He jumped up and forced his twitching body over the far side of the counter as it exploded. Bits of bearded barista blew beyond him as he slammed into the floor on the other side of the counter. His fist twitched and punched the concrete floor at full force, sending a jolt of pain up his arm. He grabbed his hand and slammed his back against the wall of the counter.

The rest of the customers streamed out of the restaurant screaming.

"I do have a remote, you ignorant dipshit!" Mildred roared at him as she pried the fork out of her hand and threw it in Kyle's direction. "And if you think I only brought one bomb here you're about to find yourself in a world of hurt!"

Kyle cradled his bruised hand as he peeked around the corner of the counter. Mildred clutched a remote detonator with her bleeding hand. In her other hand she had a small revolver style grenade launcher. The green jacket she was wearing was now open and several more explosives dangled from the straps on the inside of it.

Mildred pushed the buttons on her detonator and a napkin dispenser blew up near Kyle. He slammed into the floor as shrapnel blew past him and flaming pieces of napkin singed the back of his neck.

Kyle tried to flip over a table but his arm locked up and he had to shove it over with his shoulder. A recycling bin next to the side of the counter exploded knocking the table into him. The legs of the table grazed his chest as the surface of it pinned him into the back wall.

Mildred raised her grenade launcher.

A booming explosion sent a shower of splinters chasing after Kyle as he dove behind another table. The heat from the blast warmed his legs and quickly dissipated into the air. He did a quick pat down and didn't feel any punctures anywhere. Aside from the random muscle spasms he was doing ok so far, everything still attached so there was no need to involve the insurance company yet.

Kyle scanned his surroundings. One of the escaping

patrons had left behind a half-eaten breakfast burger; maybe he could blind her with the grease. He spotted a fire extinguisher in the corner. That would do nicely.

He pressed his cheek into the cold tile floor as he peered underneath the chairs and tables in between him and the fire extinguisher. There were no mines that he could see on any of them.

Mildred's rubber boots squeaked against the floor as she closed in on him.

Another shot rang out from the grenade launcher. There was the brief clinging of metal on metal as it struck the fire extinguisher. A thunderous explosion and shockwave followed that shook the entire restaurant and echoed off the concrete walls.

Chunks of searing hot metal leaped at Kyle and dug themselves into the back of his left arm and shoulder. Kyle screamed in agony as unfiltered pain tore into his brain. The injured muscles on his left side seized up and his arm froze.

A cooling mist of white fog followed and blanketed over Kyle. The shrapnel lodged in him chilled him from the inside. Blood dripped off his twitching fingers. He bit his lip to fight the pain. A tear escaped his clenched eyes and ran down his face. All he could see was white.

"Oh, I'm sorry. Does the little baby feel hurt now that he can't afford painkillers anymore? Don't worry, you won't feel anything soon." Mildred taunted him from the other side of the fog.

Fear crept up his spine as he realized that there was no

helicopter coming to extract him. He would not be rushed to the hospital to be put back together. If things went black here, they would stay that way, forever.

Kyle slowed his breathing and tried to regain his focus. The muscles on his left side relaxed. His body let the adrenaline fly free through his veins as he clenched his fists and his mind brought itself back under control. The drugs may have left his body but the years of training were permanently etched into his brain. His survival instincts tapped into them now. He was not about to lose to some damn skinny redhead who didn't even have any drugs in her system!

Kyle looked down at his arm to try and assess the damage but he couldn't even see his own chest in the thick fog. He carefully felt for the edge of the table with his good hand and took a quick glance over it. Nothing was visible anywhere; he was entirely encompassed by fog.

"Oh, I wonder what hashtag I should use for you." Mildred's voice slowly increased as she walked closer to him. "How about 'An asshole with a new hole'?" Mildred laughed as she cocked her grenade launcher.

Think, Kyle, think! Her voice was getting closer. Kyle realized that his only chance lay within his head. He didn't have a belt fed minigun to cut her in half with. Nobody was waiting to pick up his pieces. But the training and experience he'd gained in all of his years as an assassin had to count for something.

The Redline Burger was a relatively small restaurant. Kyle reasoned that the fog from the fire extinguisher must have filled the entire place or at least this side of it. As long as Mildred didn't open the doors or blow out a window to vent the place out he had some cover to work with. Kyle knew where his enemy was and as long as he stayed quiet, she wouldn't know where he was.

"Maybe I should just take off one of your legs and drag you back to that barstool so I can use that mine finish you off. It was Gustav's favorite after all." Mildred said as she crept closer to him.

Kyle felt around the floor with his good hand and found a piece of shrapnel that had missed him. He tossed the metal shard back towards where the fire extinguisher had been.

He stayed quiet and listened. His heart pounded against the inside of his chest.

"Are you trying to escape?" Mildred's voice moved towards the metal shard. "Well, we can't have that now can we?"

Pure unregulated adrenaline poured into his veins, and the hunt was on. Quietly he slid away from Mildred. His good arm spasmed and he had to roll on to his back to prevent it from punching the floor. Using the few muscles still under his control he slowly wormed his way behind her, keeping as low as possible.

One of the pieces of shrapnel in his arm got caught on something as he slid on the floor and an intense pain shot through him. He managed to clench his jaw and not make a noise. Heavy breaths surged out of his nose.

After dragging himself about fifteen feet, Kyle turned

and started to slide himself behind where he thought Mildred was. Part of him wondered why she hadn't just fired a bunch of grenades at him to finish him off.

He raised his head and slowly brought the rest of his body up. Three feet of fog enveloped the floor at this end of the restaurant. He was behind Mildred, who was still walking towards the metal shard he had thrown. Whatever move he made would have to be done quickly before she turned around.

Kyle frantically searched for anything he could grab. The customer who had been working on the giant aluminum framed laptop had left it in the booth next to him. It would have to do.

"You're not dead already are you?" Mildred asked the empty fog.

Kyle crouched down and slowly grabbed the laptop with his good hand. He folded it nearly closed but kept a finger in between the screen and body so it wouldn't click shut. He could feel his chest pulsing against his shirt from the intensity of his heartbeat.

"Oh, come out Kyle" Mildred said as she raised her grenade launcher to the fog.

Kyle rushed at Mildred.

His neck muscles seized up just behind her and a grunt escaped his lips.

Mildred spun around and her furious eyes met his panicked ones.

Kyle slammed the metal laptop into the side of her head. The laptop flexed and the screen cracked from the force of the impact. He saw the glimmer of one of her teeth flying out.

Mildred staggered back and dropped the detonator.

She tried to bring up her grenade launcher, but Kyle batted it down into the fog with the laptop. He smacked the narrow edge of it into her stomach, knocking the wind out of her. One of the hinges on the laptop broke free against her ribs.

Kyle brought up his leg to kick her and his first helpful muscle spasm knocked her back into the fog. He bent down into the fog and felt along the bottom of the floor until his fingers found the detonator.

Mildred staggered upright, breathing heavily. Kyle ran and dove behind the counter. He landed next to the smoldering remains of the barista.

The explosives in Mildred's jacket clinked together and rattled along the floor as she struggled to remove them.

Kyle tried to bring down his middle finger on the big red button but the muscles in his finger locked up.

"Shit!" He leaned over and knocked his forehead into the button.

All of the remaining bombs in Mildred's jacket exploded simultaneously. The thunderous explosion sent a shockwave rolling through the floor. Glasses flew off the counter and fell on top of Kyle. Various pieces of Mildred splattered against the ceiling and concrete walls. The windows of the restaurant blew out and scattered bits of glass across the surrounding sidewalk.

Kyle stood up and surveyed the damage. Half of the

restaurant had been coated in a fine red spray. One of her hands had landed in a tray of Ethiopian roast. Smoke seeped up from the newly formed crater in the tile where she had been standing.

He let out a deep sigh of relief and dropped the detonator. He pulled out his phone and took a picture of the scene for his Hitboard portfolio. It certainly didn't demonstrate stealth, but it was something.

#blownthefuckup

The upload to Hitboard completed and Kyle leaned against the counter. The adrenaline that had been rushing through his veins started to leave him. He suddenly felt very light headed and looked down towards his injured arm. Pain shot through his shoulder as his twitching neck muscles fought the command to look down.

Blood, the dark important kind, was draining down the side of Kyle's arm and dripping on to his legs. No longer the syrupy consistency it had been when he was on the hyper-oxygenating pills, the red fluid spilling out of him looked like it belonged to someone else. Indeed, he was now different on the inside. After a few moments of quiet reflection, it occurred to Kyle that the shrapnel from the fire extinguisher had gone in very deep and he needed to get to a hospital immediately.

CHAPTER TEN

Kyle's finger left a bloody smear across the screen of his phone as he started up the Charity Health app. The app linked to the vital signs monitors printed into his heart and lungs, which also helped make it a very accurate fitness tracker. Kyle had never bothered to track his fitness while he was on the pills. His current personal trainer, whom he had ditched this morning, was used to working with hippies who didn't have a dozen biometric sensors scattered throughout their body. This left all the extremely accurate fitness data his body had been collecting for the past several years completely unused until now.

The app ran an analysis and confirmed that his pulse was spiking and his blood pressure was dropping as less and less of his precious bodily fluids remained inside of him. He picked up a smoldering piece of fabric that had been part of Mildred's jacket and fought his twitching muscles to make a tourniquet around his shoulder. He jammed some napkins underneath it, and they were quickly saturated with blood. Pain shot through his left side with every breath.

He stepped outside and tried to casually walk away from the restaurant. A block away stood a sign for a private clinic; surely they would be able to help him. Bits of glass crunched under his shoes and drops of blood left a path behind him as he staggered down the sidewalk

Sterile air rushed past his face as he entered the lobby of the clinic. Blood dripped off his pants and stained the glossy linoleum floor. With wide eyes the receptionist tracked Kyle as he slowly advanced towards her. Her finger alternated between the police and janitor call buttons under her desk.

"Hello." The receptionist started off cautiously. "Can we help you?"

"Yeah, a fire extinguisher just exploded behind me..." Kyle considered explaining how this had happened. "...for no reason at all. I'm bleeding pretty badly." He held up his phone to show her his personal info. His good arm twitched and slammed the phone down on the desk in front of her. Her finger jumped back towards the police button under her desk. "Sorry about that." He took a long breath. "I don't have a card yet."

The receptionist put on a rubber glove before taking the phone from him. She looked down at the screen and immediately started shaking her head.

"I'm sorry sir, but to use these facilities you have to be a member of our company, this card is for Charity Health. They have a hospital on the other side of town. We can call you an ambulance if you would like."

"Oh come on!" Kyle felt his strength drop a little more

from the outburst. "Can't you see this is an emergency?" He took another long breath. "I'm bleeding all over your floor here."

"I'm sorry sir, but we don't have an emergency room here, just a critical care center. This clinic is strictly for members, you'll have to go to one run by your company."

"Dammit. I'm not looking for surgery or anything here, just someone to pull this metal out of me and patch me up. You have gauze and seal-all here don't you? I can pay extra for it."

"I'm sorry sir, you'll have to leave." The receptionist moved her hand back under her desk.

"Fine." Kyle relented and turned back around. On the way out he took an extra step to wipe some blood off his arm on to the wall next to the doorway.

Kyle stepped back out on to the sidewalk. His head felt even lighter. The napkins he had jammed underneath the jacket couldn't hold any more blood and it was now steadily dripping out of him and on to the concrete. Dying in the street from blood loss was not how he wanted to go out. He propped himself against the side of the clinic building and hit the 'Emergency Call' button on the Charity Health app.

The operator let the phone ring three times. "Hello, Charity Health critical care line. My name is Cynthia. How can I help you?"

"Hey! Hi Cynthia. A fire extinguisher just exploded behind me, completely at random. I'm bleeding pretty badly. Can you please send an ambulance?"

"Yes, sir, I'll get right on that. First off, I see you are calling us from our app. Can you please let me know if you have any vital monitoring implants inside you?"

"Yeah, I've got one in my heart, one in my lungs and some others."

"Excellent. Can you please say 'I do' to authorize me to take a look at them?"

"I do."

"Great sir, thank you very much."

Kyle's vitals monitor readout popped up in the app. His systolic blood pressure had dropped twenty points in the past few minutes from 110 to 90 and an alarm notification telling him to call the emergency line appeared.

"Sir. I see that you are within coverage range of one of our facilities. A drone is on the way to diagnose your injuries and determine an appropriate response."

"What? Why? I just told you what happened. I already tried to tie it all off and it's still bleeding. Can you just send the damn ambulance now?" The AIs in the cabs usually responded well to profanity. It couldn't hurt to try it out on her too.

"I'm sorry sir, but to give you the best treatment possible we need to get a calibrated diagnosis using the sensors on our drone. Drone ETA is currently two minutes. Please be patient until then."

"I can tell with my calibrated eyes that a shitload of blood has been bleeding out of me for several minutes. Now please send the fucking ambulance already!" He gulped for air. Yelling had already become strenuous.

"I am sorry sir, I didn't catch that. Can you please restate your question?" Kyle moved the phone away from his mouth and grumbled out several more profanities. "I am sorry sir, I didn't catch that. Can you please restate your question?"

"Are you fucking kidding me?" Kyle held the phone up to his face in disbelief. It had to be an AI on the phone, no human customer service rep could be this incompetent, could they?

"Drone ETA is now one minute. Please remove any tourniquets or obstructions you have over the wound site when the drone arrives. I am now putting you on hold. Please stand by." Cheesy elevator music blared from his phone.

Had it already been a minute? How long had it taken him to catch his breath?

Removing his crudely assembled tourniquet was not something Kyle had planned on doing. The request made some sense though. Once the cameras on the drone saw how badly injured he was the customer service rep would have to send him an ambulance as soon as possible.

Once the lousy drone showed up that is.

Kyle leaned against the side of the clinic listening to the soul crushingly bland elevator hold music from his phone. The twitching in his muscles was getting less vigorous as his whole body weakened from blood loss. He struggled to keep himself upright against the side of the building to keep his wound above his heart. If he lay down now he was as good as gone.

A man in jeans and a leather jacket walked past Kyle.

"Hey, can you give me a hand?" Kyle gasped out as he tried to wave down the man. The man continued walking without even making eye contact with Kyle. "Dammit."

At last the drone arrived. It hovered a few feet above Kyle and circled his body. Kyle gingerly removed the tourniquet from the wound site. With each tug on the cloth a new jolt of pain coursed through his arm. The blood had clotted to his makeshift tourniquet and ripped fresh openings in his skin as he removed it.

"See?" Kyle gasped out. "Are you happy now?" He rolled his body along the wall of the clinic, leaving a smeared line of blood on the concrete.

On the side of the drone was a bright red first aid kit. It probably contained seal-all gel or wound patches or something else that would be very helpful at this moment.

"Hey drone!" Kyle strained his eyes to look up into the main camera. "Can you drop me that first aid kit?" Sunlight reflected off the camera lens directly into his face. He had to look down at the street to keep his eyes open.

The drone did not reply. The speaker next to the array of multi-spectral imaging lenses and microphone remained silent. Only the hum of the four rotor blades was audible over the terrible elevator music coming from his phone.

All of the camera lenses retracted back into the drone and it buzzed away, taking the first aid kit with it.

The hold music stopped and the voice that called itself Cynthia came back to life.

"Sir, how did this injury happen?"

"I just told you! A fire extinguisher blew up behind me!" Kyle tried to yell louder but his body couldn't convey the rage in his mind.

"Is this a new injury?"

"Yes! I was eating lunch at a restaurant and then a fucking fire extinguisher blew up next to me, completely out of nowhere! Now I have a bunch of fucking metal in my arm and now can you please send me a fucking ambulance!" The outburst left him exasperated and he slid a few inches further down the side of the building.

"I am sorry. We do not have a listing for 'fucking ambulance'. Would you like me to send you an ambulance now instead?"

"Yes!"

"Sir, I'm going to put you on hold while I contact the ambulance driver ok?"

"Ok, can I get your extension in case I get cut off?" Immediately after saying that Kyle realized that he may have just asked a computer program for its extension. Did they even do things like that?

"Of course sir, it's 3205. I'm putting you on hold now." Cynthia said as she put Kyle back on hold.

Kyle dipped the pinky from his good left arm into the blood dripping down his right side and wrote 3205 in blood on his pants. Elevator music calmly echoed through his head as the dizziness increased.

He waited. His body was too drained to even twitch anymore. The weight of his eyelids started making it difficult for him to remain conscious. All that remained of his strength fought the urge to lie down and greet death.

A song change happened in the elevator music and Kyle checked his phone to see how long he had been waiting. Time was a fuzzy notion to Kyle's brain at this point, but he estimated that he had been on hold for at least three minutes. They had got to be fucking kidding him.

Kyle put her hold music on hold and started another call. This time he dialed her extension directly.

"Hello, Charity Health critical care line. My name is Cynthia. How can I help you?" Cynthia responded with the exact same tone that she, or it, started his first conversation with.

"Why the hell did you pick up so quickly? Shouldn't you be talking to the ambulance driver?" Kyle pleaded.

"Wait, who, oh shit." Cynthia said. She was either human or the AI programmers had left in a profane Easter egg for customers who were about to die. "Oh, I'm sorry for the inconvenience sir. I am on hold with the ambulance driver right now. It shouldn't be more than a few minutes so I'm going to put you back on hold."

"Oh, fuck that! I'm calling 911 and sending you dicks the bill!" Kyle yelled as he hung up. He then dialed 911. After telling them that a fire extinguisher randomly exploded behind him they told him that an ambulance would be there in five minutes. Survival was on the way.

Flashing red and white lights caught Kyle's attention as the ambulance pulled up. The only thing holding him up now were the bricks he was leaning on. An EMT hopped out of the ambulance and the stocky Latin man in blue came up to Kyle.

"Hi. You still need a ride or would you like to just die right here?" The EMT said in a cheery tone as he pointed to the ambulance with his thumb. Kyle nodded but didn't say anything.

"Don't worry. We'll have you at The General in a bit." The EMT said as he started to replace Kyle's tourniquet with some medical grade seal-all. A second EMT brought over a stretcher and they helped Kyle lie face down on it.

"No, Charity Health." Kyle slowly wheezed out. "Take me there."

"You sure? They don't have an ER there."

"Yeah. I'm sure." Kyle mumbled back..

"Joyce! Take us to Charity Health Main Hospital. Full sirens!" The EMT shouted to the front of the ambulance.

"You've got it Manny!" The ethereal voice of the ambulance AI responded from the speaker in the roof.

Sirens wailed and Kyle felt them picking up speed. As he watched his own blood leak out on to the floor, Kyle wondered how often they cleaned out these things.

The second EMT scanned Kyle's vitals implants and then pulled out a pack of A positive from the mini-fridge underneath the seats in the ambulance. Kyle barely noticed the needle puncture his arm as the medics started to refill his body with fresh blood. The pain of the shrapnel is his shoulder started to replace the dizziness and light headedness he had been feeling. Every bump in the road caused the metal shards to shift within him.

Refueled, his neck muscles resumed their twitching and

smacked the side of his head into the guardrail of the stretcher. The medics shot a vial of painkillers into Kyle's arm, and the bumps became more tolerable.

The ambulance arrived at the loading dock at the rear of the Charity Health hospital twenty minutes after they had picked Kyle up. Kyle looked up from the bottom of the stretcher and saw the doors of the ambulance open and the EMTs start to lift him out. Blacktop switched to gray sidewalk as the EMTs wheeled him over to the receiving desk. The guard took a look at the wounds on Kyle and scanned his thumb. A buzzing noise rang. The guard tried scanning one of his fingers instead and the buzzer went off again.

"Sir, I'm sorry but your policy has been canceled." The guard bent over, leaning close to his face. "You can't come in here."

*****

"What!" Kyle shouted using the little energy the EMTs had restored. "Hey, can you give me my phone?" He hit redial and called Cynthia directly.

"Hello, Charity Health critical care line. My name is Cynthia. How can I help you?" Cynthia was evidently not paying attention to her caller ID.

"Hey, this is Kyle Soliano. The one you wouldn't call the ambulance for."

"Oh, hello sir. How is everything going?"

"Well fuck you too. I'm at Charity Health and they're saying that my policy got canceled. You wouldn't happen to know anything about that would you?"

"Sir, it shows here that you lied on your application when you neglected to inform us about your history of domestic abuse, and your policy was canceled due to that omission."

"Domestic abuse? What the hell are you talking about?"

"Sir, your medical records show a long history over more than a decade of injuries sustained and spare parts needed due to domestic violence resulting in your injury. When you filled out your application with us, you said you had no pre-existing conditions. If you had been upfront about this history when you joined we would have increased your rate to adjust for it. Since this is not the case, we have canceled your policy."

As Kyle had just discovered, Avery listed any injuries her coworkers received on assignment as 'Domestic Abuse' on the insurance forms. Medical forms didn't have a checkbox for being injured while performing an assassination and it would have looked suspicious if all of their employees were constantly being injured on the job.

"How in the hell is domestic abuse a pre-existing condition anyway? It's not like it's something you're born with or catch in an elevator." Kyle yelled into his phone, "I can't help it if people are out to get me."

The two EMTs looked at each other and shrugged.

"Sir, anything that may cause the need for above average

care is by law a pre-existing condition. New legislation repealed the exemption for domestic abuse. It is your responsibility for making sure that your records are proper and up to date."

"Oh sure, like it's my fault." Kyle tried to move his head but was trapped by the straps on the stretcher. "People just keep blowing my limbs off and that's all on me." The EMTs and the receiving clerk shot Kyle a confused look. "Can I just pay extra now and get treated?"

"No sir, I'm afraid that is not possible. If you survive, please feel free to re-apply for insurance with us and we will give you a properly adjusted rate. Until then, thank you for your patronage." The line went dead.

"You've gotta be fucking kidding me." Kyle said as he lowered the phone away from his ear. He twisted his head up towards the EMTs and told them to take him to the public general hospital. The EMTs told Kyle that they saw this all the time as they rolled his stretcher back into the ambulance.

Insurance companies liked to put people on hold in the hopes that they bleed out before they could reach expensive emergency care. Indeed, statistical analyses of how to optimize the customer service protocols had shown that the odds of a person bleeding out increased exponentially with the amount of time the customer service rep could keep them on hold. This algorithm was internally referred to as 'Death by Politeness' and was developed by Harriet Nidrah, a former presidential statistician who had also developed algorithms for calculating acceptable losses.

Harriet was now retired and living on a tropical island paid for with the hush money she had earned from her work as a consultant.

"Those sons of bitches, they tried to kill me" Kyle mumbled as the ambulance took off.

"Alright if I tap your phone on this panel to pay for this ride? Seeing as how your insurance isn't going to pay for it." The EMT asked as he waved Kyle's phone at him.

It was another twenty minutes for the ambulance to go back across town before it pulled into the parking lot of San Francisco General Hospital. Now that all of the private Emergency Rooms had been renamed to 'Critical Care Centers' in order to exempt them from having to accept undesirable patients, The General was the only remaining public emergency room in town. The bare concrete walls of the main structure loomed over the ambulance as it passed underneath to the ER receiving area.

The security guard at the door pulled a fresh checklist off the wall and took a look at Kyle's gauze and blood covered back.

"Is he conscious?" The security guard asked the EMTs.

"Yes."

"Is he stable?"

"We stopped the bleeding and gave him a refill of blood and some painkillers so he isn't critical anymore but he'll still need surgery to get all the shrapnel out of him."

"Ok, take him to the waiting room. First door on the left." The guard said as he motioned towards the doorway. Kyle realized he should have pretended to be unconscious to get quicker service.

The remnants of the never ending battle between lemon and pine scented cleaners assaulted his nostrils as the stretcher rolled into the waiting room. A nurse poked her head down to look Kyle in the face, her red horn rimmed glasses almost falling off in the process.

"So, what happened to you?" The nurse asked.

"A fire extinguisher blew up next to me." An exhausted Kyle replied.

"Hmmph. That's a new one." She didn't sound impressed as she stood up and talked to the EMT some more. Kyle could hear the EMTs saying something about his insurance and the nurse complaining about how they always got all the rejects on her shift.

The nurse popped her head back down to Kyle's level, now holding a tablet computer in her hands. "Before we can do anything, you'll need to fill out this application for public insurance."

"Why do I have to apply for it if it's public? Why can't they just add it to my taxes or something?"

"Because we need to know how much you make to figure out what to charge you."

"Yeah, my taxes wouldn't help at all there." Kyle tried to roll his eyes at her, but couldn't manage it in his weakened state.

In Kyle's case his taxes would not have been entirely accurate anyway as he officially only made minimum wage at his previous company. All the rest of his money was in a secured account in a bank in Singapore, the Switzerland of the east. This combination of low taxable income and his lofty apartment and living standards had led the IRS to flag him as a potential male escort in their database.

"Come on. Look at me." Kyle tried to gesture towards the gaping wounds in his shoulder with his head. "I don't have time for all that."

The nurse took a look at the patch job that the EMTs had done. "That's just a trickle, we have mops. You have plenty of time. You're in line behind all of those people." The nurse pointed over to the side where Kyle could see a gunshot victim, a woman holding a kid with a runny nose, a person who appeared to have cut off his foot with a hedge trimmer and a drunk with a towel over his finger humming to himself.

"The kid with the runny nose is ahead of me? I just had a fucking bomb go off behind me."

The nurse looked disapprovingly at him and didn't say a word. Kyle relented and went back to staring at the floor.

"Fine, but I'll need someone to help me fill it out. My arm is all screwed up and I'm stuck in this thing."

"What about your other arm?"

"Oh, that one's fine."

Before he could finish his sentence the nurse clamped a tablet to the front of the stretcher and adjusted it so that it was staring Kyle straight in the face. She then lowered the side of the stretcher next to his good arm.

"If you need help reaching your wallet or anything just let one of us know. Here is your number and a pager if you need help." The nurse said as she hung a number and a pager from the sidebar of the stretcher. Kyle felt like he was a prized cow about to be auctioned off.

"How long?" Kyle dared to ask.

"You've probably got about three hours, plenty of time to fill out all the forms. Don't you worry."

"Ugh." All he could see through the hole in the bottom of the stretcher was the application form on the tablet a foot away from his face. The floor around the periphery of his vision moved as the nurses wheeled him into a corner of the waiting room. Before leaving they secured a thick vitals monitor to his good arm, presumably so they could bump him to the front of the line in case he started to die.

The tablet was fully enclosed in a blood red rubber case to make it harder to tell if it hadn't been cleaned recently. The first page of the public insurance sign up form beamed at him in a shower of far too cheery pastels that clashed with the blood red rubber surrounding them.

The first screen asked 'Individual' or 'Small Business' and Kyle wondered how many small businesses wound up in the ER. He reached down and poked Individual.

The next screen asked him to select his state. He poked California from the list and the tablet took him to an entirely different website. Why the hell didn't they just start him there from the beginning? Don't they know what state they are in? He became convinced that these extra steps were just to waste time so the wait didn't seem so long.

Kyle proceeded to slowly enter his name, phone number, email, address, social security number and all sorts of other dry information one letter at a time by finger poking the screen with his good hand. No more doubt about it, this was definitely just to make the wait seem shorter.

After entering a full page of personal information the tablet asked him if he would like to apply for coverage, just in case there was some other reason he was filling out forms for an insurance application.

Employment status came up next. Kyle started to try to remember what his cover job had been, but then remembered that it didn't matter now anyway. He checked the box for 'unemployed'. It was the first time in nearly two decades he had told the truth on one of these things.

The tablet asked him for an emergency contact. He stared at the screen for a full minute. Kira was the only real option, but if they notified her she would find out that he hadn't listened to her. Reluctantly, he typed in her information. Whatever she did to him, it couldn't be worse than winding up face down on a stretcher in a dank public hospital.

After punching in some more personal information Kyle was greeted with a bright blue screen telling him that he was not yet enrolled with a little button in bottom corner that said 'Enroll Now'. Kyle wondered if whoever made this was paid by the page.

A tutorial video popped up showing in colorful illustrations the differences between the four types of coverage he could pick from. With each new plan the bar for the deductible went up as the bar for the monthly payment went down. Kyle poked at the screen to try to get it to skip but the animation continued uninterruptible for a full minute.

At last the video stopped and a list of thirty-six different options appeared on the screen.

"What? Thirty-six? Dammit." Kyle cursed as he scrolled through the options. He had mistakenly assumed that the public option meant one option, not thirty-six of them. As he read the details of each option as he realized that there were at least three different companies listing plans with varying amounts of deductibles and monthly payments.

This wasn't public insurance, this was a lame publicly run insurance shopping website.

Not one of the options said anything about cosmetic or performance enhancing drug coverage. All of these plans were the rental cars of health insurance. You probably wouldn't die in one, but you would have to roll down every window by hand.

Kyle's eyes grew heavy as he looked over the list of health plans. The adrenaline that had been supercharging his veins had completely vanished. The painkillers had numbed away the searing pain from his injuries. He managed to get five sentences into the detailed description for one of the health plans before passing out. Visions of the Charity Health headquarters engulfed in flames and the burning staff of the customer service department jumping out of the windows filled his dreams.

CHAPTER ELEVEN

Something poked Kyle's right arm and interrupted his dreams of retribution. He groggily opened his eyes and checked out his surroundings. He was in a hospital bed with blank grey sheets. There was no TV in the room. A skinny man in blue scrubs was poking his arm with the same tablet he had been looking at when he passed out.

"Ah, Mr. Soliano. You're awake, excellent." From his badge, Kyle could see that he was a NURSE. "You didn't finish filling out the application before you passed out, but don't worry I'll leave your tablet right here." The nurse placed the tablet in Kyle's lap.

"What? Oh, dammit." Kyle mumbled as he looked down at the tablet and remembered where he was. The lingering mixture of drugs in his system still fogged his mind. He was exhausted. His left side ached all over and could barely move at all.

"You're in the outpatient wing. You just got out of surgery from, let's see here..." He looked down at the pen and paper clipboard attached to Kyle's bed. "Ah, you had multiple pieces of shrapnel removed from an exploding fire extinguisher. Hmm, that's a neat one. How do you feel?"

"Like crap, my shoulder hurts like hell. What kind of crappy printer did you guys use to make this arm?"

"Printer? You're in The General man, we don't have printers here." The nurse let a quick laugh escape as he looked over the chart. "But, we did remove the shrapnel from your arm and all the wounds have been sealed up with bio-adhesive so as long as you don't try yoga or anything until you've fully healed they should remain shut and you should be fine. We called your emergency contact while you were out. I'll tell her she can come in."

Oh crap. They had called her. Kyle tensed up in preparation for the verbal beating he was about to endure.

The nurse walked back into the room with Kira right behind him. She examined Kyle and the support equipment tied to him. Kira had long wondered what would happen if she ever quit taking the pills.

When cosmetic enhancing pills first came out on the market, everybody thought they could be young forever. The first generation of users wound up dying or losing their minds from degenerating neural pathways as they aged. Their minds knew how old they were even if their outer appearance didn't show it. After much investigation, newer pills were developed to re-coat the myelin sheaths covering neurons in the brain to prevent this in future customers. Kira had already started taking the myelin pills, but nobody knew what part of the human body would wear out next on such an elongated lifespan.

Seeing a preview of what could likely happen to her sent a chill down her spine. She gulped and sat down in the chair across from Kyle's bed.

"Well, you're a sad sight. What happened?" Kira asked.

"Another assassin. Turns out some ninja put out a hit on me and is recruiting people who have something against me to close it out." Kyle replied. He looked at the nurse to see how he reacted but he just continued checking vitals as if this was no different from any other conversation he had overheard on the job.

"What ninja?"

"I don't know. I blew up the assassin with some of her own grenades so I didn't get a chance to check her phone."

"Well, at least we have some idea of who is after you. Congrats on your first kill as a freelancer. Did you at least remember to take a picture?" Kira said as her eyes traced back and forth across Kyle's hairline. Had more of his hair fallen out now too?

"Yeah, I got it." Kyle replied. She still wasn't making eye contact with him.

"Good. I'm impressed you were able to keep your wits about you in that situation. I was starting to worry you had lost your killer instinct. How do you feel?"

"Like I'm in someone else's body." Kyle's shoulder spasmed and jerked his head to the side. He fought against it and after a few seconds was able to turn back towards Kira.

"What was that?" Kira asked in an alarmed voice. She looked deep into Kyle's eyes. "Is that what happens when the pills start wearing off?"

"No, it's from..." Kyle's words trailed off and he took a deep breath. She was going to hate this.

"You're friend has some bad synthetic enzymes in his blood stream." The nurse casually mentioned from the corner of the room.

"Thanks, asshole!" Kyle yelled at the nurse.

"You did what!" Kira jumped out of her seat and loomed over him. "What the hell were you thinking? You idiot! You don't have any idea what was in those things!" Her fist clenched on the edge of his pillow. Kyle sunk back as far as he could to try and keep the pillow behind his face and not on top of it.

"I know, I know. It was a dumb idea. I get that." Kyle protested.

"You're fucking pathetic you know that. You can't even go two days at a gym without resorting to black market drugs?" Kira leaned over him and pointed up at her raging face. "I shouldn't even be wasting my time trying to help you. I'm glad I tossed that old sniper rifle of yours. You don't deserve to have it back."

"From what we can tell, the effects look to be temporary. He'll just need to avoid meat for three or four weeks until all the enzymes get flushed out of his system." The nurse chimed in again with a smile on his face.

"What?" Kyle yelped. He stared at the nurse with his jaw gaped open.

"Oh, really?" Kira's mood shifted completely at this new news. Now her face was awash with delight. "Just think of all the salads you'll be enjoying." She giggled.

"He also had a lot of shrapnel is his left arm and shoulder from an exploding fire extinguisher. We removed all that and patched him up. The bio-adhesive should help to close the wounds in about two weeks, but it'll be at least six weeks for the internal damage to heal up before he can do any strenuous activity again."

"Six weeks of rest and salads." Kira said as she savored every word. "It's like a dream come true isn't it?"

Kyle remained stunned.

"Don't forget to fill out the rest of that application or you can't leave. Oh, and you both need to leave in thirty minutes, so tick tock and all that. Buzz me if you need anything." The nurse waved as he left the room to go torture some other poor bastard.

"You have got to be kidding me." Kyle sighed.

"Like you don't deserve it. That's what you get for not listening to me." Kira said as she relaxed back down in her chair.

"Ok, I'll admit it. I didn't listen to you and I'm sorry." Kyle pleaded. He looked down at what remained of himself in the hospital bed. "I'm sorry I ignored your advice, but I really need your help. Can you please help me?"

Kira leaned against the back of her chair and considered Kyle.

"Well, you did survive a fight with an assassin despite your body having to deal with black market drugs messing everything up. That's something. You haven't forgotten everything I taught you. Maybe you aren't a completely hopeless cause." She walked over to Kyle and looked him straight in the eyes. "Ok, I'll help you, but I have a few questions first. Are you willing to do exactly what I say?"

"Yes." Kyle nodded. Every rookie Kira had ever trained for the past fifty years always answered the same way.

"Are you not going to eat another cheeseburger until I say that you can?"

"Dammit." Kyle paused for a second. He bit his lip but he knew that there was no other way. "Yes. Yes, I won't eat another cheeseburger until you say it's ok."

"Good. When I think you're ready we'll find a job that you can take on solo, without any enhancements. If we can find a good one to pad your resume we should be able to get you a new job."

"I have a thought about that actually." Kyle said as he grabbed his phone off the table next to his bed. "Let's see if I can find a Hitboard listing for Cynthia. She was the support rep who cancelled my coverage."

"You know she's probably just an AI right?"

"AIs don't usually cuss like that." Kyle punched Charity Health into the search field but nobody named Cynthia showed up. "Dammit, nobody by that name." He looked at the list and noticed something strange at the top of it. "Oh, hello, her boss has a listing. Sindrin Malik, CEO of Charity Health."

"CEO of a major national corporation, that's always good. So this is the CEO of the company that dropped you when you dared to actually use their insurance. I like it. How much is the client offering?"

"Clients, plural. It's crowdfunded." Kyle scrolled through the list of clients attached to the Hitboard posting.

"Really? I didn't know they allowed that." Kyle handed Kira his phone and she examined the long list of clients who had contributed to the hit request. "Wow, it's like a total list of sob stories on this thing. Look at this, one guy posted five hundred bucks to this hit after spending the rest of his money trying to save his wife. Here's a family that posted the ten thousand they weren't allowed to spend on surgery for their daughter." Kira stared at the rest of the listings and went silent.

"Something wrong?" Kyle asked. Kira usually didn't stay this quiet for long.

"Nothing wrong. It's just been a while since I had anything close to a moral high ground on a job."

"Well, technically I'm the one taking the job. You'll get the assist of course. Even with all your references an extra thousand satisfied clients couldn't hurt I'm sure."

"Yeah, whatever, I'll try to keep you from killing yourself during this one."

"And while I'm taking him out, I'll see if I can track down who Cynthia is and where she lives."

"Kyle, drop it. You'll never find her, even if she is a real person. What would you do if you found out it was just some automated AI? Kill the programmer? Kill the person who supplied the voice? It wouldn't accomplish anything if there isn't a hit posted for her anyway."

"I would feel better."

"True. But wouldn't you feel even better if you got a job

that hooked you up with the good pills again? Then you could spend your time eating cheeseburgers when you aren't eating out girls with glow in the dark pubic hair?"

Kyle considered this for a moment.

"Good point." He nodded in agreement.

"That's better. First we need to get you healed up and back in shape while we figure out something special for Dr. Malik." She handed the phone back to Kyle.

"He's not a doctor." Kyle corrected her as he brought up the profile on his new target.

"What? Really? How is he in charge of a health insurance company?"

"Says here he was an investment banker who found a way to screw over people even more by switching to health insurance."

Kira sneered.

Kyle felt much better about his chances.

"Well in that case, we'll have to figure out something special for *Mr.* Malik."

CHAPTER TWELVE

"Well, what kind of health plan are you looking for?" Avery responded over the phone the following morning.

"The kind where I don't have to get approval for everything and where they can't drop me on a whim and leave me to die." Kyle replied.

"Hmm, well that rules out HMOs."

"No shit."

"You should probably go with a preferred provider option, a PPO. That way you can just pay for whatever you want as you go."

"And I can go anywhere?"

"You get a discount for staying in network and depending on the one you pick they may not cover out of network visits but you won't have to get approval from anyone to see a specialist."

"So I can get new limbs and drugs whenever I want? Why didn't you tell me about this before?"

"Wait till you see the bills. Getting a new arm and a leg will probably cost you the other arm and leg." Avery chuckled.

"Wonderful."

*****

Kyle returned to the gym two days later with a freshly printed arm and shoulder newly attached. The surviving half of his old dragon tattoo was now completely gone and replaced with fresh pale skin. Well defined lines indicated the border of new skin along his chest and back where the new parts had been grafted on.

Avery had been right about the cost though. This latest appendage cost him a month's mortgage and he was down to seven months' worth of cushion in his bank account. If he kept taking hits like this every time an assassin showed up, he would need to move to somewhere cheaper while he looked for a new job.

"Hi stranger. Welcome back." The old man at the reception desk greeted him. "Should I call up Reuben for you?"

"No, thanks though. I just had a bunch of surgeries and my arm is feeling a little stiff. Who you got for yoga here?" Kyle inquired.

"Glow would be perfect for you." The old man nodded and looked over Kyle. "She's got a class in twenty minutes. Room 2"

"Sounds good." Kyle signed in and headed to the class.

Kyle came back to the desk an hour and a half later, drenched with sweat and breathing hard. His muscles felt flexible and energized but his soul was completely drained.

"You didn't..." He sucked in a breath. "...tell me that was a hot yoga class." Kyle told the old man.

"You seemed like you could handle it." He smiled and leaned over to Kyle. "Feel better now don't you?"

Kyle nodded.

Glow, the short French yoga instructor with long brown dreadlocks walked up to the desk. Her spiderweb patterned clothes were covered in as much sweat as Kyle was but her soul remained intact.

"Feeling ok? Glow asked. First time is always the hardest."

"Yeah, I'll live. Great class, by the way. Totally kicked my ass." Kyle wiped sweat off his forehead. "Sorry about farting in it. I've been eating a lot of vegetables lately."

"No worries. That is a natural scent and I am glad you were able to fully relax your body to the point where it could reconnect itself to nature."

Kyle opened his mouth to reply, but then changed his mind and shut it. Instead he just nodded and headed for the door.

The next morning Kyle went to the gym and headed right up to the old man at the reception desk.

"Ah, twice in a row now. Trying to get a streak going?" The old man lifted an eyebrow at Kyle. "What'll it be today?"

"I need a refresher course on grappling. Throwing

people. Using their own weight as leverage against them. Judo, Jiu-Jitsu, Eskrido, that sort of thing. Kyle replied with a determined smile. Got anybody good for that?"

"Hmm, I believe I do." The old man thumbed through the catalog on his desk. "Oh my. Yes, he should be able to work you good." He looked over Kyle's body. "I think Somboon is free right now if you're willing to pay for a private session."

"I am. Private would be good."

Kyle headed over to the training mats. A skinny old Thai man who was just a few inches shorter than Kyle was re-racking some wooden staves. His white hair stood out against his black gi and sun-drenched skin.

"Excuse me, are you Somboon?"

"Yes, you are Kyle? Why are you not wearing a gi?" The instructor finished putting the staves away and turned towards Kyle.

"Oh, I just wanted to try you out first before I invest in one. It's been a long time since I did any of this so I'm looking for a refresher course."

"Ok, let's see what you have to work with." Somboon gestured for Kyle to come closer to him. The Sifu put his hand on Kyle's neck. Kyle instinctively countered by putting his hand on Somboon's neck. In a single swift motion, Somboon ducked under Kyle's arm and put his shoulder into Kyle's lower chest. He then flung Kyle over his shoulder and on to his back on the mat.

"You will get a gi if you want to train with me." Somboon calmly stated as he pinned Kyle face down into that mat with his foot.

"Yes! I will get a gi!" Kyle responded emphatically as his nose was squashed into the mat. "Ok?"

The following morning Kyle arrived at the reception desk at his usual time. The old man was once again on watch as Kyle came in.

"You got a nice little routine going here." The old man said.

"Thanks. I'm sorry I didn't introduce myself earlier." He held out his hand. "Kyle Soliano."

"Hank Teevan, nice to make your acquaintance." Hank sat up a little more straight in his chair. Did he purposefully not wear a name tag to try and strike up conversation? "So what'll it be today?"

"I need a sparring instructor slash partner for kickboxing practice. The more aggressive the better."

"Hmm, well we got a gal named Vileena who teaches a class and helps train the MMA wannabes in the evenings. Come back around six and she'll be here. You could probably convince her to do a private tutoring session, but she's damn tough."

"Does she break bones?" Kyle asked with a straight face.

"No, not that I've heard of. Probably can't with the pads on."

"That'll have to do."

Kyle made his way to the ring inside the gym later that day. About twenty students wearing tight fitting clothes lined the perimeter of the ring. In the center wearing blood red padding with bright teal workout clothing peeking out from underneath stood Vilenna Pereyra. Her light brown curls with magenta highlights protruded out from the gaps in her helmet. Faint traces of UV reactive tattoos textured her cheeks and neck.

He volunteered to spar against her to start off the class. She let him take the first shot at her and he lightly hit her stomach pads.

"Don't hold back. I'm padded, so you can't hurt me. Hit me as hard as you can!" She yelled at him.

Kyle threw all his strength into the next punch at her ribs. The padding absorbed all of the impact. Even at full power he couldn't hurt somebody with pads on. A few weeks earlier he would have liquefied most of her internal organs with a hit like that. He really was just a normal human now.

He pondered this for a moment instead of keeping track of where Vileena's legs were going. She swept his legs out from under him and brought her heel down into his chest while he was in midair. The blow drove him into the floor of the ring and left a bruise underneath his padding.

"Now class. That is why we will be working on footwork tonight." The surrounding crowd nodded vigorously in agreement.

*****

"So this is where you've been coming? It's not as dirty as

I thought it would be." Kira said as she surveyed in the interior of the gym.

Four weeks of salads and his new workout routine later, Kyle was a changed man. Most of the remnants of drugs in his system had been flushed out. His skin was no longer self-tanning and the hairs on his body had gotten long enough to stop itching all the time. His newer limbs were still distinct from the rest of his body, but they had grown darker while the rest of him had gotten lighter.

"Yeah, it's not too bad. You get used to the smell after a few days." Kyle replied.

Desperate for meat, Kyle had taken a chance and eaten some bacon in his fourth week. He went a full hour without twitching before he dropped a weight on his foot at the gym. After three weeks of being a vegetarian, having to deal with the occasional muscle twitch was still totally worth it to be able to eat meat again.

The pain limiting pills had completely worn off and now everything he touched felt a little different. It was a strange sensation, becoming un-numb to one's self. Even touching the snooze button on his alarm clock every morning felt more real to him somehow. The notes on the boxes of the pain limiting pills stated that they wouldn't affect smaller impulses, but that appeared to have been an overstatement.

Glow had told him that this was his body reawakening its harmonic connection to the earth and that he should not be afraid. Kyle decided he probably shouldn't tell her anything personal ever again.

"I'm ready." Kyle said as he watched two old hippies in

sweatpants finish up in the ring.

"You sure? It's only been four weeks. You really think you can survive a sparring with me?" Kira raised her eyebrows.

"Yeah, let's do this." Kyle said as he started putting on his sparring gloves and pads.

"Alright, you asked for it." Kira taped towels around the pads on her legs and arms.

"So what's this challenge you brought?" Kyle tightened the straps on his helmet.

"I'll show you in the ring." An unmarked paper bag sat on the bench next to Kira.

"So this is the friend you've been training for?" Somboon asked. Rueben stood next to him.

"Yeah, going to put that training to the test." Kyle replied. Somboon looked Kira over and nodded to her.

"You have a fan club now?" Kira lightly elbowed Kyle's arm.

"Something like that." Kyle tightened up the straps on his legs.

The two gray beards left the ring. Kyle and Kira stepped in.

Kira walked over to the stool in a corner of the ring and opened up the bag. She pulled out an enormous cheeseburger sweating with grease and set it on top of the stool.

"Is that what I think it is?" Kyle asked. His nostrils opened as wide as possible to take in the aroma.

"Oh this? It's some sort of bourbon bacon cheeseburger

from that Kokumi place you keep talking about. I thought it might give you some good motivation." Kira said with a grin.

Kyle's nose confirmed that it was indeed his favorite type of burger.

"So, if I knock you out I get to eat it?"

"Kyle, please." Kira said with a chuckle. "You have no chance of knocking me out with those wimpy base model arms of yours. Your challenge is to get to that cheeseburger without dying or getting seriously hurt. Now, do you think you can get past me?"

Kyle gazed at the cheeseburger sitting on the stool. The fragrance of the still warm burger called out to him like a siren's song. His body flooded with adrenaline as all of his organs teamed up to work together to win the burger.

"Damn right I do. Let's do this!" Kyle shouted as the adrenaline kicked into his system. He started hopping in place.

"Ok, on three. One, two, go!" Kira shouted.

Kyle charged right at Kira and took a swing at her head. She ducked his swing and with a forceful shove of her enhanced arm flung him backwards into the ropes like he was made of packing foam.

The ropes caught Kyle and rebounded back, launching him right at Kira. His feet flew just above the ground. He extended his toes down as far as he could to try and ground himself but there was nothing to push off of.

"Dodge!" Somboon yelled.

Kira's knee slammed into Kyle's chest. Two ribs gave

way as her knee knocked the air out of his lungs. He ricocheted off her knee and fell face first to the mat. Blood sputtered out of his mouth as he tried to push himself up. Kyle rolled on to his back and gripped his chest as he gasped for breath.

"Oh shit!" Reuben exclaimed with his mouth wide open. "I'll go get a towel!"

Somboon covered his face with his palm and walked away.

"Well, that was just pathetic." Kira said as she walked over to Kyle's squirming body. "You only lasted about five seconds against me. You're going to have to do better if you really want to eat one of these again." Kira took a big bite out of the cheeseburger directly over Kyle's face. "This thing is so gross. I don't see why you even like them." She took another slow giant bite.

Hot bourbon tinged grease dripped down on to his face. He licked what precious grease his tongue could reach off his cheeks.

"Do you really have to eat that right over my face?" Kyle complained between labored breaths. "You've already hurt me enough for one day. It's going to cost a ton to fix this."

"Why?" Kira said as she took another big bite and chewed it slowly. "Does this make you mad?" She tore a piece of the burger open with her teeth. Hot grease and cheese oozed down on to Kyle's forehead.

"I hate you so much right now." Kyle spat more blood on to the floor of the ring. He looked to his side and saw Reuben holding up towels and a bottle of cleaning agent.

"Good. Another try next week then?" Kira said with a smile as she licked bourbon sauce off her fingers.

"Damn right."

*****

A week later Kyle was ready for a rematch. Word of Kyle's next match with Kira got out to all of his instructors. Rueben, Somboon, Vileena and Glow all showed up to watch their pupil spar against the curious woman who only came to the gym when she wanted to beat him up.

"Remember what we worked on." Vileena shook his shoulders.

"Try not to die!" Somboon stated flatly. "Our insurance goes up if we have another fatality."

"Please don't talk to me about insurance." Kyle replied as he shook his head.

"What other fatality?" Reuben asked. Somboon smiled, then turned around and took a seat on the bench. Reuben shrugged and followed him.

"You ready?" Kira asked from the ring. She tightened the tape holding the towels to her gloves.

"Hell yeah! Let's do this." Kyle roared as he leaped into the ring. "I even had some carne asada last night and no twitching at all."

The two of them tapped gloves and then put their fists up. Kyle felt the rough texture of a towel brush his face as he evaded a kick to the head. He countered with a series of punches to her chest.

The nerve capping pills in Kira's reinforced body reduced the pain from even the mediocre amount of force Kyle's arms were now limited to producing. The filtered signals informed Kira's brain that she had just been repeatedly tapped with a feather.

She threw a punch at his stomach and he swerved in close to avoid it. He shoved his shoulder into her to try and get leverage but he couldn't get a good grip with his gloves on. Kira flung him to the ground with a shove from her arm.

He rolled to avoid the crushing impact of her heel coming down and sprung back up.

"Nice recovery!" Vileena clapped.

Kira kicked high and Kyle ducked low underneath her leg. He tried to slide his leg behind her standing leg but the thickness of his pads got in the way. He leaned back into her outstretched leg and she leaped around him to catch herself.

"Decent improvisation." Somboon commented without a hint of emotion.

Kira overextended with her next punch and Kyle responded with a strike aimed for her chest. As his arm neared full extension a muscle spasm shot through his elbow and redirected the punch directly into Kira's face, right in between the pads of her helmet. Kyle's eyes bulged out of their sockets. They had agreed on no headshots.

Kira growled and socked Kyle right in the face. His body

went airborne and twirled around twice. Teeth rained down on the ring as blood flew everywhere. Kyle landed on his back. He tried to scream but blood ran down into his throat and choked him. He turned on to his side and another tooth fell out as he coughed up blood.

"Fuuuuck!" Vileena gasped out. Rueben and Glow sat stunned with their mouths gaping open.

"Remember not to die." Somboon shook his head and walked away.

"How do you plan on eating cheeseburgers without any teeth?" Kira took a bite out of the hickory tequila burger she had brought. "Have you had enough? Maybe it's time to just give up on this whole thing." She looked down on his writhing body.

"No." Kyle spat out another tooth. "Next week." He let some more blood drain out of his mouth. "I'll be the one eating that burger."

CHAPTER THIRTEEN

"How did the interview with the people in Oakland go?" Kira asked over the phone.

"Not well." Kyle switched her voice over to his printed in headset so he wouldn't have to keep holding his phone up. "They also thought I looked a lot smaller than in the pictures. They said they didn't think I could take out a target without hurting myself in the process."

"That sucks. At least this headhunter Darren is finding openings for you."

"Yeah, I guess." Kyle looked out the window of the cab. It was a nice sunny day out. Not a cloud in the sky. "I even brought my pistol with the suppressor on it and some throwing knives to show off with. So much for that."

"How was the vibe of the place?"

"Small, their front is a fancy cupcake shop that only takes appointments."

"That sounds like really bad camouflage."

"It is. They must have had four people knock on the door asking to buy cupcakes while I was there. They also had this dopey looking guy at one of their desks who kept staring at me."

"Did he know you?"

"I don't think so. I ran a facial recognition scan on him and he's just some assassin named Trevor. He didn't show up in my history or anything."

"Well it sounds like you probably lucked out on not getting picked up by that place. There's still a lot of the day left, want to go ahead with our next sparring match anyway? It could help you get some aggression out."

"No, not today." Kyle rubbed the bottom of his new jaw. "How about tomorrow instead? Maybe you could not leave me with a giant hospital bill this time?"

"Hey, that's on you. Do better and I won't break anything."

The cab slammed on its brakes. The sudden stop threw Kyle into his seatbelt and his head snapped back into the headrest.

"Pedestrian detected." The cab AI said in a soothing deep British accent.

"What the hell?" Kyle turned and looked out the front window of a cab.

A person wearing bright blue power armor was standing in front of his cab.

The Yavelhoff XP304 full body powered exoskeleton battle suit was a compact model by modern power armor standards. The snug armor plating was only two inches thick, allowing the user to be able to fit inside normal hallways and doors while still providing excellent protection against small arms fire. This particular model was equipped with a rocket pod on the right shoulder and a belt felt machine gun connected to an ammo drum on the back. The outer titanium skin of the armor had been painted bright metallic blue. This color scheme was worthless as camouflage, but it did help catch the eye of soon to be victims to make sure they saw death coming.

The armored foe aimed his machine gun at Kyle's cab.

"Oh shit!" Kyle yelled as he ducked to the floor of the cab. Machine gun fire roared out and shattered the windows of the cab. Bits of glass rained down on Kyle. The cool fragments of glass sliced across his skin and they showered down on him.

"Kyle! What's going on?" Kira shouted into his ear.

"Another damn assassin out for me!" Kyle yelled back. He whipped out his pistol and blindly fired a few shots over the front seat of the cab. The hollow point rounds scraped the paint off the power armor but couldn't penetrate through the plating. "The asshole is wearing power armor. That's so not fair!"

"It appears we have entered a region of civil unrest." The car calmly stated. "Shall I flee?"

"Yes! Go!" Kyle yelled at the cab. The car swerved around the armored assassin and sped up. The assassin shot out the rear tires and the car scraped into the edge of the sidewalk in front of a park. The top of Kyle's head banged into the door.

"Oh, don't try to run Kyle. You'll ruin the framing of my video." An unknown voice spoke into Kyle's ear through his headset.

"What the fuck?" Kyle exclaimed.

"Who was that?" Kira asked.

"I'm the one who is going to kill you. Please stay in the car. This will look great."

Kyle peeked up over the back of the seats. The cover on the rocket pod dropped down exposing the yellow tips of six rockets.

Kyle opened the door and leapt out of the car. A rocket burst through the giant hole in the shattered rear window and slammed into the dashboard. The explosion engulfed the car in a giant fireball. Flaming shreds of upholstery floated in the air around him. He jumped to his feet and ran for the trees. The man in the power armor leisurely walked after him.

"Kyle where are you?" Kira asked.

"I'm in Lake Temescal Park!" He shouted back as he ran.

"Got it. You can do this!"

"Go ahead and run. I can see everything you see and hear everything you hear." The raspy voice said.

"Who the hell are you?" Kyle yelled back. Bullets whizzed through the air around him and tore into the trees. He ran through splinters and sawdust as he went deeper into the park. A pair of runners on the nearby path screamed and rushed away from him.

"I'm an assassin with Sam's Sweets. The company you interviewed with this morning. I hacked your phone while you were in our office. You connected to unsecure Wifi and now you will pay the price."

"Wait, are you Trevor? That dopey guy at the desk?" Kyle paused behind a tree. He reached his gun around it and blindly fired a few more shots in Trevor's direction.

"Yes, how do you know my name?" Trevor stood still for a moment. "It doesn't matter. You'd never be of any use to us without the pills, so I figured I might as well collect the bounty on your head to pad my stats." Trevor fired another rocket at the tree Kyle hid behind. It blasted a hole through the trunk only a few feet above Kyle's head.

Kyle crouched, his hands over his head as splinters rained down on him, sticking in his hair and scratching up his face. Splinters covered his entire body. He wiped away the bits of wood blocking his eyes, got up and dashed across the moist dirt towards the lake.

A delivery notification popped up in his eyes only display. Kira had sent a care package. Whatever it was would arrive in two minutes.

"Getting pizza delivered for your last meal are we?" Trevor commented over Kyle's earpiece.

Kyle wove a random path in between the trees. Bursts of machine gun fire shredded apart every tree he passed. A white marker appeared in his field of vision at the edge of the lake. The drone had picked a clear spot to land. He dove over a rock and made a beeline to the drop point. He could hear the low rumble from the jets of the high speed delivery drone getting louder as it approached.

"Oh, I don't think so." Trevor opened fire at the drone. Bullets cut an engine off and the drone spiraled downward.

The package broke free. The large metal case banged off a tree and smacked into the soil just ahead of Kyle. The flaming drone crashed into the lake. "You know Kyle, you can never be anything other than a target without the pills. Me, I have skills."

Kyle charged towards the metal gun case ahead of him. What had she sent him? A belt fed rocket launcher? A secret prototype plasma rifle? A small tactical nuke?

The case identified his phone as he got closer. An unlocking notification popped up in his vision. The latches on the sides of the case spun around and unlocked. One side opened up and the contents lifted into view.

She kept it!

He dove over the case and grabbed the dark green sniper rifle. His fingers reunited with the custom printed grip. His hand reflexively pulled the bolt back and cocked a fresh .308 round into the chamber. A huge smile spread across his face. He rolled across the ground and scurried behind a large boulder.

He only had the clip in the gun. Only eight shots to save himself with.

Kyle flicked the powered scope on. The battery was charged and the electrodes in the grip were feeding into a heart rate monitor that worked in conjunction with a series of piezoelectric actuators to cancel out any instability from his heart beat. The zoom worked.

"Why so angry? Are you suffering from erectile dysfunction?" Trevor laughed into his ear.

Pop-up ads began to spam all over Kyle's eyes only

display. He couldn't see anything but ads for penis pills and porn with farm animals.

"Can you see this, motherfucker?" Kyle waved his extended middle finger in front of his face.

Unfortunately, Trevor's video feed only showed what Kyle could see and not a filtered view of it so he couldn't actually see that Kyle was flipping him off. His picture in picture merely showed the edges of a hand waving behind a lot of pop-up windows.

Kyle desperately reached into his pocket and felt for the power button on his phone. He squeezed down on the button. His eyes only display vanished. The low background hum from his printed in headset went quiet. The air around him was still.

Trevor crunched his way towards him. The suit he was wearing whirred slightly with each step. Powered battle suits were made for frontal assaults, not stealth. Kyle poked the end of his sniper rifle out from around the rock in the direction of the crunching noises. Slivers of blue armor floated between the bark of the trees. A shiny blue head appeared.

Kyle locked his sights on Trevor's head and pulled the trigger. A thunderous bang burst from the front of the rifle. The end of the gun jumped up. Kyle pulled it back in to his shoulder, tighter than before.

The bullet hit Trevor square in the chest. His sights were off. He ducked behind the boulder and adjusted his scope down a bit.

"You see. I barely even felt that. You can't break a

Yavelhoff suit with a piece of crap gun like that." Trevor shouted with the loudspeaker on his suit. He opened fire on the boulder Kyle was hiding behind. Chunks of rocks blew off and rock dust drifted down on to Kyle.

Kyle made a run to a group of trees. Bullets sliced through the air around his head and took off the top of one of his ears. He ignored the pain as he slid behind a tree.

Thankfully, only the cartilage in his ear had been damaged. Replacing that part of his ear would not require anesthesia and could be done by simply adhering a new piece to what was left of his ear.

The tree creaked as bullets tore chunks of bark out of it. Kyle lay on the ground and peeked his gun out around the base of the tree. He fired another shot. The rifle kicked up as the bullet sliced through the air into Trevor's right hand. The impact knocked Trevor's aim off to the side. Branches cracked and fell from the tree next to Trevor as his machine gun fired wildly into the air.

Kyle fired another shot. The bullet severed the belt feeding bullets into Trevor's machine gun.

The machine gun fired a dozen more rounds. Shots echoed throughout the park.

Clicking replaced gunfire as the gun ran dry.

"You know what? I don't even need this." Trevor bellowed and tossed his gun to the ground.

Kyle zoomed out a bit until could see all of Trevor's upper body. The cover on the rocket pod lowered, exposing remaining rockets in the pod. He fired another shot.

The bullet slammed into the tip of one of the rockets, detonating it inside the launcher. The explosion spread to the three other remaining rockets. The shockwave knocked leaves from the surrounding trees to the ground. The explosion echoed off the boulders in the park and drowned out all other noise. Kyle felt the rumble through the soil.

A smoldering Trevor lay on the ground on his back. The force of the blast had peeled open his armor from his right shoulder down to the middle of his chest. An opening in the bottom of his helmet exposed his chin and neck. Flames from the blast had scorched his armor black.

Kyle approached him slowly. The blast had fractured Trevor's collarbone and part of it stuck out of his skin. Blood ran down his chest and neck.

"Never be a real assassin, huh?" Kyle put a foot on Trevor's chest and jammed the barrel of his sniper rifle into the bottom of Trevor's jaw. He tilted the rifle until it pointed up into his skull. "Looks like your company only hires losers, no wonder they didn't want me."

"Please. Please." Trevor trembled. "Anything you want!"

"Do you have your phone on you?" Kyle asked.

"Yeah! Yeah! It's in the left pocket on my leg. Just slide the lock back."

"Ok." Kyle kneeled down. "Try anything and I take your damn head off." He unlatched the armored pocket and took the phone out. "What's the code?"

"5318008. No tricks. Believe me." Kyle tried the code and the phone unlocked. He checked the status indicators and didn't see any heart icons on the top.

Kyle opened up Trevor's Hitboard app and looked up the hit request for him. He started recording a video to post to the hit message thread.

"Hi there. I'm Kyle Soliano, the target of this posting." He spoke into the front facing camera. "I'm here to let you know that if you are thinking about taking this job, you're going to end up like this asshole. So leave me alone!" He turned the phone around so the camera faced Trevor.

"Wait! Wait! No! Please!"

Kyle pulled the trigger. The bullet blew through Trevor's jaw, up through his brain and slammed into the inside of his armored helmet. The force of the impact tore Trevor's head away from his neck and drove it into a nearby tree.

The report from the shot echoed and silence followed it.

Kyle forwarded the video to his own Hitboard account. Perhaps Sam's Sweets would reconsider now that they had an opening?

#rifleuppercut

He looked up the requestor of the hit. It was a ninja. Kyle could tell from the black facemask he wore in his profile picture. He recognized the golden eyes peering out from behind the mask.

Diego Hitomoshi, asshole ninja of the Hideki clan, had somehow figured out who he was and put a hit out on him.

CHAPTER FOURTEEN

"Impressive work taking down that assassin in power armor with nothing but a tiny sniper rifle." Kira said as she placed a fresh whiskey pepperjack cheeseburger from Kokumi Burger on the stool in the corner of the ring. "Did you decide to wait to get your ear fixed so you could get a bulk discount at the hospital?"

"Ha ha, no." Kyle scoffed. "But I do think I've got something good in store for you." He placed Trevor's phone next to the cheeseburger.

"Whose phone is that?" Kira stretched her arms.

"Our dearly departed Trevor. He's got a direct line to Diego since his Hitboard account is linked to the posting for me. I figure a little taunting will be in order after I beat you today. I'm sick of that guy sending lackeys after me. It's time I call him out." Kyle left his sparring pads and gloves on the bench and headed into the ring unprotected.

"Interesting approach." Kira said as she smiled at him. "Do you think it's worth the risk of taking a shot from me with no padding?"

159

"I need the speed." Kyle hopped around the ring. He nodded to Somboon, who was sitting on the bench outside the ring. "And I need to be able to grab you." Somboon nodded back.

"I'll go get the mop." Reuben walked away from the ring.

Glow and Vileena had declined to watch this bout. Seeing Kyle beaten into a bloody pulp once had been enough for them.

"Alright. Let's see if it works." She said as she stepped to the center of the ring and bumped fists with Kyle.

Kira took a swing at his shoulder and Kyle slid out of the way.

She kicked for his chin but Kyle ducked away from it. He then pulled her outstretched foot forward to try and get her off balance. Kira fell backward but caught herself and flipped back up.

"You've gotten better." She said encouragingly.

"Somboon and I practiced extra hard this week." Kyle smiled at her.

Kira charged at him and tried to hit him with a left hook. Kyle dodged the punch and leaned forward and down. Using Kira's own momentum against her, he lifted her over him and flung her into the mat behind him.

"So I have him to thank for this." Kira roared as she flipped up back to her feet.

Kyle made a dash for the cheeseburger. If he could just touch it he would win.

He felt the warm air near the cheeseburger with his

fingertips. He was so close. Just a few more inches.

Kira's foot slammed down into the mat in front of him. The towel wrapped around her leg grazed his fingertips as it blew past. The force of the impact clanged off the metal supports and shook the entire ring.

Kyle quickly reeled his arm in and hopped a few steps back.

"You're going to have to do better than that." Kira positioned herself directly in front of the cheeseburger and raised her arms.

They both stood still, eyes locked, analyzing each other's positioning.

Kira charged Kyle.

A towel wrapped fist launched out at his shoulder. He spun his chest away and pushed into the side of her arm. He slid in close and brushed his leg up against hers.

Kyle leaned his weight into Kira. Reflexively, she pulled her leg up to counter Kyle, but that left her off balance on one side. Kyle pressed his body weight into the side of her shoulder. Kira's shoulder gave slightly under the pressure. It was time to strike!

He pivoted behind Kira and shoved the bottom of his arm into the back of her head. Kyle then hopped on to her back and landed his full body weight on her. Unable to pull her limbs in fast enough, Kira slammed face first into the mat. Kyle followed up by immediately jumping on her back to buy a few precious fractions of a second.

A six foot tall Samoan jumping on someone's spine would typically cause a loud cracking sound as the victim's back broke. Depending on their insurance they would either have to undergo an expensive and long spinal replacement procedure, or live the rest of their life paralyzed. Neither of those outcomes would be considered fair play for a friendly sparring match. Kira however, never played fair, and Kyle was well aware of the punishment her body could take. Instead of the snapping sound they expected, Somboon and Reuben only heard the thud of Kira's stomach hitting the mat as her reinforced bones and muscles absorbed the impact.

Kyle ran for the stool as fast as he could. Reuben cheered him on. He made it to the corner and grabbed the cheeseburger. The bun was still warm and the sauce oozed out all over his hand. He lifted the cheeseburger and held it up like a trophy.

Behind him Kira still lay face down on the mat, laughing. She rolled over and started making muffled claps for him with her towel covered hands. Rueben started clapping as well. Somboon nodded his approval and walked away.

"You devious little shit. It's good to have you back." She said with a warm smile. Kira got up and walked over to him.

"Does this mean you aren't going to hurt me?" Kyle asked cautiously. The delicate intermingling of the pepperjack and whiskey had already worked its way up to his nose. He wouldn't be able to resist it much longer.

"Maybe." Kira said as she pulled the towels off her arms and legs. "What did you learn?"

"That I can't survive frontal assaults with people

anymore." Kyle paused for second to think about it some more. "That I need to evade and use their strength against them? Take them out without taking any shots in return."

"That's good, you pass. Go ahead, dig in." Kira nodded towards the cheeseburger.

Kyle grabbed the plastic knife out of the bag. He cut it in half.

"Thanks for knocking some sense in to me." He handed Kira half of the cheeseburger. He took a huge bite of his, the pepperjack scalding his tongue in the most delicious manner.

"Congrats on beating an eighty-five year old woman." Kira saluted him with her half and took a bite.

Kyle's eyes went wide but his mouth was full of burger. He swallowed quickly and wiped the whiskey sauce off his lips. "Really?"

"Yeah, I told you I have a lot of experience in this business." She savored another bite of cheeseburger. "You just got fat and hairy when your pills wore off. I don't plan on finding out what happens to me if I go cold turkey. Go call out your ninja buddy, but try to push out the day of your duel. We got a CEO to deal with first."

Kyle nodded and finished up his half of the burger. Every bite tasted like victory. A bomb of pure deliciousness landed in his stomach. He shimmied his way back to Trevor's phone. Kyle logged back into Trevor's Hitboard app and left a message for Diego.

"Hey, asshole, I'm going to be out of town for a while so you can stop sending your little minions after me. If you want me, let me know what day would be a good day for you to die and come get me yourself!"

CHAPTER FIFTEEN

Crisp morning air filled Kyle's nostrils in Chicago. He sat on a concrete park bench across from the Charity Health building. From this bench he had an unobstructed view of the main entrance. Their headquarters was located in a relatively small forty story skyscraper in downtown Chicago. He also had a clear line of sight to the Originals Gus' restaurant down the street. They were one of the top fifty cheeseburgers joints in the country. They hadn't opened up a location in the San Francisco bay area yet so he had never tried them before. That restaurant would make an excellent victory dinner location.

Kyle had scoured the internet for pictures of Sindrin Malik and loaded them into the facial recognition app on his phone. He had also looked up who his admin was and instead found that Charity Health had converted all of them to unpaid internships in order to save money. How efficient of them.

James Loffen had posted in large bold letters on his social media accounts how he had landed the gig as Malik's personal intern for the summer. James put his published papers and highly regarded university economics classes to work fetching coffee and food for his boss every day. In an age of automated delivery drones, a live human minion was the highest form of status symbol. Kyle's facial recognition app scanned everyone who came or went from the building, looking for both of Malik and James.

It was 8:57am. If James kept to the same schedule he had the past two days he should appear in exactly one minute to fetch Sindrin Malik's coffee from the Sundeer coffee shop across the street.

Kyle hadn't taken any metallic weapons that the sentry robots might detect with him on his flight over. Instead he had emailed himself copies of the files needed to print out weapons at the local PrintStop. Despite the warnings against printing weapons all he had needed to do to get around the safeties was rename the files so that they didn't sound like weapons. His throwing knives became TURTLEHATS and his custom contoured silenced pistol assembly had become a YOUTHSOCCERTROPHY. Bullets still needed to be purchased on site but it would be impossible to trace a gun that didn't exist until the week it was used. After a few short hours with the metal laser sintering printer in the store Kyle was fully armed and ready for action.

Kyle readjusted the fully loaded YOUTHSOCCERTROPHY hiding under his jacket and watched the entrance intently. The clock in his HUD clicked over to 8:58am. Still no James.

The ninja, Diego, never responded to Kyle's challenge. Kyle assumed that he had wussed out and gone back under whatever rock he crawled out from. He could always go find him later after he got a new job.

At 8:59am James came out and headed across the street. The facial recognition app buzzed and drew a circle around his face. Sunlight reflected like fire off his red curly hair. He must have caught a slower elevator down this time. Kyle would have to account for that variability.

Eight minutes later the intern exited the Sundeer with two cups of coffee in hand. One with one checkbox on the side and the other with many options checked. After a few steps, James took a sip from the cup with only one checkbox. Kyle smiled. The kid was consistent.

There was no need to wait until the end of the day, so Kyle headed back to the hotel he and Kira were staying at to prepare for tomorrow's hit.

*****

Kira and Kyle sat on concrete benches on opposite sides of the park. The SpectreSight Z150 multi-spectral scope of Kira's micro-minigun bulged against the sides of her messenger bag. Neither of them knew the exact layout of the inside of the building, but considering that there was only one security guard in the lobby one minigun should be sufficient for an escape.

Kyle adjusted the collar on his blue tie. It was 8:50am. His inoffensive, subdued beige business suit blended in with the school of dull suits that flowed around him. He nervously ran his fingers down the slight bulge in his suit left by the 3D printed throwing knives. Satisfied they hadn't slipped out, he readjusted his tie and locked his gaze back on the entrance.

A delivery drone set down on the pond next to Kyle and unfolded its solar panels. Kyle closed his eyes and took a deep breath.

"Nervous?" Kira's text popped up at the bottom of his eyes only display.

"Well, I wasn't until you went and jinxed me." Kyle responded through his printed in microphone. He let a smile slip out and waved to her.

"I've got your back if you need it. Good luck." Kira spoke reassuringly into his ear.

Eight minutes later an alert triggered in Kyle's vision. The intern had just exited the building and was heading to the coffee shop, just like he always did. Kyle got up off the bench and walked towards the coffee shop. He adjusted his pace so that he would arrive at the door to Sundeer just ahead of James.

"Oh, I'm sorry, please go ahead." Kyle said to James as he cut in front of him. Kyle held the door as the young man walked in. He stood about a foot and a half shorter than Kyle. The ends of his loose fitting sleeves came all the way down to his knuckles.

"No, I'm sorry." James shook his head vigorously as he

stared up at Kyle. "Go ahead, you were first."

"Thank you very much." Kyle said with a fat grin as he went inside.

Kyle ordered a salted caramel mocha and then stepped into the waiting area. Lifeless zombies awaiting their fuel stood motionless around him. He towered over all of them. Even without the pills puffing out his muscles he was still the tallest person here. Kyle nodded to some of the faces as he stepped behind them, but they were all too focused on waiting for their orders to pay him any attention.

James placed his order and then joined the crowd of zombies by the pickup counter. A barista called Kyle's name and he picked up the steaming hot mocha and sipped it just behind James. He peered down at him like a vulture. The intern was busy examining a bunch of photos posted by a girl named Simone and he remained completely oblivious to the giant Samoan sipping a mocha right behind him.

"James!" Announced a barista. Kyle watched him go to the pickup counter and take a tray of four drinks.

Four drinks! What the hell was going on? Kyle furiously sipped his mocha as a shiver went down his spine.

Two of the large cups had several checkboxes written on the side of them, but which was the CEO's order?

James made his way towards the door with the tray. Kyle bumped his arm with his stomach. The intern let out a gasp as he bent over and tried to save the drinks. Kyle placed his large hand over the tops of cups to save them. None of the other people waiting for coffee budged. They were all so groggy that even searing hot coffee wouldn't get them to move.

"Oh my, sorry. I'm so sorry." Kyle said as he helped steady the tray while James got back up. "That was almost really bad."

"Thank you." James sighed in relief. He took a sip from one of the smaller cups. No poison for that one.

"Hey, you work at Charity Health right? I just started there. I'm Neal, I work over in accounting." Kyle extended his hand in a friendly gesture.

"Oh, um, yeah." The volume of James' voice increased to nearly confident levels. "Yeah, I work there. I'm Mr. Malik's personal assistant." He stressed the 'personal' part. "James Loffen, you can call me Jimmy." He shook Kyle's hand.

"Jimmy, so very nice to meet you." Kyle reached into his pocket and grabbed a quick dissolving poison strip. "Out picking up drinks for our boss?"

Kyle had spray coated his fingers with a thin layer of plastic earlier in the morning. This allowed him to safely handle the poison strips in his pocket and ensured that he didn't leave any fingerprints anywhere.

"Yes, this latte is his favorite." Jimmy nodded to his right, a cup with a ton of checked boxes on it. That must be the one.

"Well, I'm sure he'll be very glad you didn't drop it." He locked eyes with Jimmy and slipped a poison strip through the opening as he tapped on the lid. Kyle was about to add a lot of satisfied customers to his resume.

"Which school do you go to?" Kyle asked as he followed Jimmy out of the coffee shop.

"University of Chicago. I'm studying economics." Jimmy stood up a little taller as he said so.

"Awesome. I'm a Yale man myself. I was a male cheerleader when I wasn't learning the numeric arts as I trained to achieve my destiny as an accountant."

"You were a cheerleader?" Jimmy asked in disbelief.

"Oh yes, I'm very good at throwing people." Kyle nodded emphatically back.

"I believe it." Jimmy replied as they entered the Charity Health building. Kyle held the door for him.

Kyle confirmed his suspicions about Charity Health's level of security as they entered the lobby: barely any existed. A lone security guard sat a desk to the left, far away from the three receptionists at the main desk in the center. Given the number of people who had put a hit out for the CEO of this company, Kyle was surprised to see no angry customers in the lobby aside from himself.

The security guard glanced at Jimmy and waved him through. He didn't even bother to put his tablet down to look at Kyle. To him, he was just another suit.

Kyle slowed his pace slightly to allow Jimmy to get to the elevators first. They were wired with security panels that required a keycard in order to open them up, just like his apartment building.

"Oh, I haven't gotten my card yet since I just started. This is really embarrassing, but could you please call the elevator for me?" Kyle asked in his most innocent voice.

"Sure, no problem." Jimmy tapped his card to call the elevator.

Did nobody here follow standard security measures? Was this really the first time that an assassin had infiltrated this place? So many people want the boss of this place dead and his own intern just buzzes in people he doesn't even know? Why was this kid so damn friendly anyway? Kyle shook his head but he couldn't shake off the feeling that this was somehow a trap. It was almost certain, that when they reached the top floor the doors would open and the cybernetic guard dogs with chainsaw teeth would jump him. He switched his drink to his left hand and brought his right closer to the gun under his jacket.

They stepped into the elevator. Kyle's heart raced with excitement. He bobbed up and down. He sipped his mocha.

Adrenaline and caffeine flooded his bloodstream. Soon he would have a new job and all the cheeseburgers that went with it!

Jimmy hit the button for the fortieth floor. Straight to the top, just like Kyle had planned.

"I always figured you were a cheerleader in a past life." Kira's text popped up.

Kyle shook his head back and forth as the elevator ascended. He loosened up his neck and shoulders. It was time to go to work.

The elevator doors opened and a large bald man came up to Jimmy as he stepped out.

"Ah, you've got the coffee. Great, now our meeting can

finally start." The man gestured to Jimmy to follow him. Kyle kept his distance a step behind them. "Which is the one with the espresso shot?"

Jimmy pointed to the cup Kyle had planted the poison in. The man grabbed the cup and took a deep swig of it.

Shit!

Kyle screamed on the inside. He gritted his teeth and clenched his fists. The poison strips had a delaying agent on one side, but that only gave him an hour before the poison took effect and a large bald man suddenly dropped dead somewhere in the building.

"Ah, that's the stuff. Thank you Jimmy. I'll take the rest of these into the meeting. You go fill up Mr. Malik's mug. You know he doesn't like to go a minute without a cup of joe within arm's reach."

"Yes, Mr. Velk, I know." Jimmy looked down and nodded. "I'll go get it ready right away." Kyle let out a sigh of relief. He turned the corner at a break in the line of cubicles.

Kyle tapped his phone and started a one hour timer in his HUD. He grabbed a manila folder out of an empty cubicle and held his cup to his lips as he walked down the row of cubicles parallel to Jimmy. Keys clacked away as phone calls in different corners of the office overlapped with each other. The cubicles here were standard office cubicles, metal frames covered in thin fabric. The offices lining the walls had solid wood doors and gold engraved name plates.

Kyle watched Jimmy's red hair move over the top of the

cubicle walls. The intern made his way towards a corner room with closed doors. Then he turned around and walked back across the length of the room to an office with double wooden doors. Kyle orbited him and peered down the hallway he had just walked down. Jimmy opened the double doors and walked in.

The CEO's office didn't require a security card or even have a lock on the door. These corporate jobs were too easy, he should do these more often.

A few moments later Jimmy came back out with a blue mug in his hand. Kyle covered his face with the manila folder and tracked the red hair to the break room at the opposite corner from where Kyle was standing. He followed the path Jimmy had taken. The name etched in gold next to the double doors confirmed it, Sindrin Malik CEO.

Kyle leaned against a filing cabinet as he watched Jimmy put the mug in a coffee machine and load fresh beans in. The intern punched the start button and headed for the bathroom. The coffee grinder started whirring.

Kyle slowly walked towards the break room. He peeked around the corner as he crossed through the doorway and saw two women chatting by the microwave on the other side. He pressed his lips to his cup and waved the folder at them. One waved back but didn't bother to turn her head.

He stood directly in front of the coffee machine. The grinder stopped. Kyle put down the folder and pulled out his spare poison strip. He scraped the time delay agent off the back side by pressing it between his thumb and the edge of the countertop. The hairs stood up on the back of his neck as he fought to control his breathing.

He dropped the strip in. It dissolved quickly as hot coffee was poured on top of it. Without the time delay agent the poison would take effect in about five minutes after Malik drank from it.

Kyle checked over his shoulder. The two women were still chatting. He picked up his manila folder and wiped the white time delay agent off of the counter with it. He then slowly turned around and walked back out of the break room. He dropped his cup down from his lips and positioned his hand on the bulge from his gun. He held his breath and walked.

Back in the hallway he allowed himself a controlled exhale. He scanned the floor. The conference room door was still closed. Office drones continued pounding away at their keyboards and thanking people for their help over the phone around him.

Kyle walked back towards the conference room and checked the nearby cubicles and offices. Along the wall perpendicular to the conference room was an empty office with the lights out that faced the backside of a row of cubicles. He peeked into the office and saw that it was completely bare aside from a desk and a monitor, so he stepped into it. The large window in the office let the morning light in so it wasn't completely dark, but it would have to do. He looked out through a crack in the doorway at the conference room door. It was still closed.

Something slammed into the back of Kyle's shoulder

and knocked him face down into the floor.

CHAPTER SIXTEEN

The force of impact knocked the air out of Kyle's lungs. His lips rubbed against the fuzzy carpet as he sucked air back in. The body armor under his suit absorbed most of the hit. The hit bruised him but nothing was broken and he wasn't bleeding.

Illinois was not in Kyle's new PPO coverage area. Kira would have to drag whatever was left of him to Ohio for treatment if any serious injuries occurred here.

Kyle quickly rolled to his side and leapt to his feet.

Standing beneath a hole where a ceiling tile had been removed, was a man in a gray business suit with a pink shirt and tie. A thin tanned strip of skin surrounded his golden eyes.

"Tell me." Diego said in a hushed voice. "Do you have any idea how much of a mess you made?" The ninja smiled as he pulled out a black machete from underneath the back of his suit.

"Why did you send those assassins after me instead of coming yourself?" Kyle pulled out his gun and a throwing knife. His eyes locked on to Diego's golden eyes.

"I've been busy cleaning up the mess you made after killing my master." Diego whispered angrily. "Now I will avenge my honor." Diego pointed his machete towards Kyle.

"Come and try." Kyle whispered back. He took aim with his silenced pistol. The ninja stepped to the side and slammed the machete into the gun. Kyle wasn't strong enough to resist Diego and keep his aim on point. He pulled the trigger and a burst of three bullets quietly exited the building via the glass window.

Diego stepped in close and sliced upwards with his machete. Kyle jumped backwards, saving his neck, but putting his back against the wall.

The ninja rushed at Kyle and swung the machete for his head. Kyle ducked as the machete carved into the drywall above him. He then dove across the empty desk and rolled to the opposite side of the office.

Kyle got to his knees and then brought up his silenced pistol and steadied the gun with his other hand as he aimed at Diego. Five shots hit nothing but wall as the ninja dove out into the hallway. Kyle hopped back to his feet and chased after the ninja. He turned through the doorway just in time to see Diego do a backflip over the cubicle wall and disappear.

Kyle peeked out the door and checked both sides to make sure nobody was watching. He took off his jacket and draped it over his gun. He picked up the empty folder he had left on the desk and put it on top of his jacket. Sweat seeped through the sides of his shirt. Cautiously, he took a step out of the office.

Sounds of typing and bland phone conversations enveloped him once again. His pulse quickened and he scanned every nook and cranny as he walked out into the hallway. He walked past the conference room Malik was in, the door was still closed and he could faintly hear voices laughing inside of it.

He slowly walked down the hallway and peeked into every office and cubicle he went past. The employees of Charity Health all had perfect skin and none of them wore glasses. It was good to be in charge of your own health plan.

"Oh my god!" A woman in one of the cubicles yelled. Kyle rushed over and spun into the cubicle, pistol at the ready. "Isn't he so cute?" A woman with curly blonde hair held up a picture of a baby on her phone.

"Yes, very." Kyle backed up and lowered his jacket. A man in the neighboring cubicle leaned over the wall and started making 'Aww' sounds. Kyle shook his head as he turned and walked around the corner to the middle row of cubes.

A door opened. Kyle's ear perked up and his head spun around towards the conference room. The door to that room was still closed. A man stepped out of the office two doors down from it and headed towards the elevator. Kyle kicked the floor and took a deep breath.

"You can take this ninja, just keep calm. You can do this!" An encouraging text from Kira popped up in his vision.

He rounded the corner and started walking in between the third row of cubicles and the break room. A man with black hair and a gray suit walked just in front of him. Kyle crept up behind him and checked his collar. A sliver of pink poked out just beyond the collar of his gray suit.

Kyle steadied his gun and aimed for the back of the man's neck.

"Morning Eliot." A large man carrying a breakfast burrito said as he waved to the man in the gray suit.

"Good morning Larry." The man responded back with a deep, husky voice. Kyle froze and lowered his gun back down. "That's a nice breakfast you've got there. Try not to smell up the whole floor this time ok."

"But this one has three kinds of cheese, who wouldn't want to wake up to that?" Larry laughed as he passed by Eliot and went into the break room. Eliot went into a cubicle and Kyle walked past him. Kyle shook his head as he glanced at the man's face and confirmed he wasn't a secret ninja.

Kyle turned the final corner at the end of the hallway. Malik's office was directly in front of him. A series of filing cabinets lined the wall in between the CEO's office and the break room. Three beeps came from the break room and the low hum of a microwave followed. He walked up towards Malik's office.

A machete shot out through the side of the last cubicle and sliced the bottom of Kyle's tie off, narrowly missing his chest. He jumped to the open side of the cubicle with his gun at the ready. Diego leapt over the cubicle wall and landed behind Kyle.

Kyle spun around and ducked Diego's machete as it whizzed over his head. He rolled away from then ninja towards the filing cabinets and tried to get a bead on Diego with his pistol. Diego slapped his machete up into the barrel of Kyle's gun. Kyle lost his grip and the gun flew up into the air. Diego snatched it out of the air and slammed the gun down into the open drawer of one of the filing cabinets and kicked it closed.

"How did you know I was here?" Kyle dropped his suit jacket and pulled out two throwing knives.

"The admin ninjas at Hitboard told me you'd taken this mission. So I assumed I would find you here." Diego hacked away at him. The machete scraped against one of Kyle's knives as he deflected each strike.

"Fucking ninjas." Kyle shifted his body and elbowed the flat side of the machete, knocking it into one of the filing cabinets.

He quickly stabbed Diego in the hand with his other knife. The ninja dropped his machete and Kyle kicked it under the bottom edge of the cubicle in front of him. Diego reached back under his jacket and pulled out a smaller knife. The ninja slashed at Kyle's arm. Kyle tried to block with his two throwing knives but his arms collapsed against the ninja's strength. Diego shoved Kyle and flung him back into a filing cabinet. Metal handles jammed into the back of Kyle's ribs leaving a deep bruise.

The doors to the conference room opened and a group

of people poured out of it. Kyle and Diego checked the direction the office workers were heading then silently nodded to each other and backed up into their respective corners. Diego hid his bloodied hand behind his back against the side of a cubicle. The ninja placed his foot on top of the machete handle that Kyle had kicked away. Kyle tucked his knives back into his pocket and stepped next to the filing cabinet his gun had been thrown into.

Over the tops of the cubicles Kyle could see a group of heads coming towards him. He kept an eye on Diego as he felt the front of the drawer next to him for a handle. His fingers felt the change from painted metal to the cold bare metal of the handle and pulled it open. He reached in and felt around for the gun. His fingertips touched the edge of the custom printed grip but the gun had fallen under some folders and he couldn't get his hand completely around it. Kyle's heart thudded against his bruised ribs as he tried to get a grip on the gun.

A circle appeared in Kyle's vision highlighting the top of Sindrin Malik's head. Kyle watched him enter his office alone out of the corner of his eye. Two of the other employees walked in between Kyle and Diego.

"Good morning Maya." Diego said cheerfully to the woman. She gave him two quick glances then nodded back to him. He grinned at Kyle. Kyle sneered back.

The two Charity Health employees turned the corner. Kyle reached deeper into the filing cabinet but couldn't get underneath the folders to grab his gun. Diego kicked his machete back up to himself and snatched it out the air. He brought the machete down as he tried to slice off Kyle's arm at the elbow. Kyle yanked his arm back out of the filing cabinet and pulled his knives back out. Kyle elbowed the drawer shut, catching the bottom edge of Diego's machete inside it. He then made several quick stabs into Diego's arm and leg. The knives went in cleanly, without any metal on metal scraping as they pierced Diego's skin.

Diego kicked at Kyle's head. He sidestepped the blow and the ninja's foot pounded a dent into a filing cabinet. A loud clang rang through the office. The two of them froze to see if anyone noticed.

A few tense heartbeats later, office chatter and phone calls resumed.

Kyle jammed his knife into the side of the ninja's leg and held it as Diego pulled it back, drawing a dark line of blood from his calf to his ankle.

The microwave in the break room beeped several times. Diego pivoted to shield his wounded side. Kyle backed away from him towards the break room.

Someone approached from the break room. Kyle nodded again to Diego. He held his machete behind his bloody leg, and Kyle tucked his knives up his sleeves. Both combatants breathed heavily.

The aroma of three kinds of freshly nuked cheese preceded Larry's arrival in the hallway. Kyle nodded to him as he went by. As soon as Larry passed Kyle, the muscles in Kyle's arm spasmed and he punched Larry in the back of the head. The hungry office worker crumpled face first to the floor. The breakfast burrito narrowly escaped being crushed by its incapacitated owner and landed a few inches in front of him.

"Shit!" Kyle exclaimed in hushed voice. If someone saw Larry's body, he was screwed. If Larry woke up and he was still standing here, he was screwed. If he spent any more time fighting this damn ninja, Malik might die before Kyle could prove he was the one who poisoned him, and this whole trip would be for nothing.

"What the hell did you do that for?" Diego yelled at him as quietly as possible.

"I didn't mean to!" Kyle replied in a very loud whisper. He flung a throwing knife at Diego's head and the ninja batted it away with his machete. Kyle made a mad dash for the cabinet holding his gun. Diego swiped at him with his machete. Kyle ducked under it and tried to deflect the blade with his knife.

The force of the slash knocked Kyle off balance and he tripped over Larry's body. The throwing knife slipped out of his hand as he landed face down on top of Larry. The scent of three kinds of molten cheese flooded his nostrils. Diego raised his machete with both hands on the grip, its tip down, ready to slice through both men.

Kyle grabbed the breakfast burrito. The outer crust singed his hand as he rolled over. Kyle crushed the burrito. Three kinds of searing hot cheese and molten egg substitute burned his hand as they blasted out like a volcano erupting into the face of the ninja. Diego let out a yelp of pain as the contents of the breakfast burrito scalded and blinded him. The ninja dropped his machete and clawed desperately at his eyes as he tried to wipe the molten mixture off of his face.

Kyle dropped the burrito and grabbed his throwing knife. He clasped Diego's mouth shut. Then he jammed the knife through the ninja's eye and twisted it around to liquefy his brain. The muffled screams stopped as the ninja's body went limp.

"Are you alright over there?" A woman asked from the next row of cubicles.

"Oh. Yeah. Just almost spilled my coffee. Had quite a scare there." Kyle hoped the woman was too lazy to look over the cubical wall. He pulled the knife out of Diego's eye and slid it back under his jacket.

Kyle shifted the weight of Diego's body onto his and dragged the corpse to the cabinet his gun was in and retrieved it. Rearmed, Kyle carried the body to Malik's office and opened the door.

"What the hell is that?" Malik shouted as he put down his blue coffee mug. Kyle dropped the body in front of him and slammed the door shut.

*****

"That." Kyle caught his breath and rubbed his bruised ribs. "Is a ninja." He shoved the body into the bottom of the door with his foot. "I am so, so glad you aren't dead yet." Kyle took a picture of the dead ninja with his eye camera and posted it to Hitboard.

#threekindsofdeath

"Nice one on the ninja!" Kira's cheered him on over his earpiece. "Now off this guy so we can go grab a cheeseburger!"

"Was he here to kill me?" Malik asked with a trembling voice. His body was perfectly enhanced. The only trace of his fifty-three years was a line of gray hair intentionally left at the bottom of his gelled black hair for that distinguished look women go for. His body was strong and muscular but not as huge as Kyle's had been. It was good to be the CEO of a health insurance company. He probably set his own prices for the pills.

"No." Kyle paused for a second to think of how to phrase things. "He wasn't. But I am."

"What!' Malik reached for the phone on his desk. Kyle blasted it apart with a round from his gun. Malik froze and put his hands up as Kyle aimed the silenced pistol at him and walked over.

"Good. Keep them up." Kyle peered down into the blue mug as he got close to the CEO's desk. The coffee in the mug was half gone, now it was just a matter of time.

"Why are you doing this?" Malik begged as beads of sweat formed across his forehead.

"Because you assholes dropped me and left me for dead." Kyle growled in response as he leaned over Malik's desk. Malik's eyes widened and his lips twisted as he struggled to come up with a response. "And I'm not the only one. A lot of people and relatives of the people your company left to die want you dead. So today, I'm helping us all get our revenge."

"Money?" Malik stuttered out the words with each gasp of breath. "I have lots of money. Whatever it takes is yours."

"It's a little too late for that Sindrin." Kyle pulled out his phone and attached a mini-tripod to it. He started to frame up a good shot for the camera. "I already poisoned your coffee. Now I'm here to photobomb your death so I can get my revenge, collect the bounty and pad my résumé."

Malik's gaze turned to his coffee mug. His whole body shuddered. He opened his mouth, but only managed to eke out a croaking noise. He grabbed his chest and desperate eyes locked on to Kyle.

There was no time to set up a good shot for his phone camera. Kyle quickly toggled the front facing camera on and kneeled down next to the chair Malik was sitting in. The CEO looked up and saw his own panic stricken face reflected back to him on the phone's screen.

"Hi everyone. This is Kyle Soliano. You may remember me for my work in Burkina Faso or the Caribbean and may have been skeptical that I would be a good fit for your organization." He smiled as he pulled out a piece of paper from his pocket and unfolded it. "Well, here to show you that I can strike like a silent force of nature is Sindrin Malik, CEO of Charity Health." Kyle held up the unfolded piece of paper next to his phone for Malik to see. The faces of twenty-eight other Charity Health victims looked down on the quivering face of Sindrin Malik. "As you can see, I even do 'last thing you see' requests."

Malik's jaw gaped open but his lungs couldn't push any words out. His eyes rolled upwards and his face fell on to his desk. His tremoring body went still.

"If you want subtlety, you want Soliano!" Kyle winked at the camera and stopped the recording. "It's done. I got it." Kyle said to Kira, who was still listening in.

"Nice. I'm glad he died when he did, I was worried you were going to keep monologuing."

Kyle added a starry border to the video and posted it to the front of his Hitboard page. He hit the big 'Job Complete' button for the Sindrin Malik listing on Hitboard. A fat grin expanded across his face as he applied the hashtag.

#solianomeanssubtlety

Kyle packed away all of his weapons and took a large folder of paperwork off Malik's desk. He pushed Diego's body aside with his foot as he stepped out of the office and back into the hallway. A woman with blonde hair and a lavender pantsuit walked towards the CEO's office.

"You should give him about twenty minutes. He just got on a call."

"Again?" The woman grumbled and turned away.

To his left Kyle saw three Charity Health employees trying to wake up Larry. Now was a good time to leave.

Kyle made his way back to the elevator and hopped in as the doors closed. He punched the button for the lobby and pulled off the remaining half of his clip-on tie.

As he exited the lobby of Charity Health, Kyle pulled

out his phone and took a celebratory selfie in front of the building.

#nodrugsnoproblem

CHAPTER SEVENTEEN

Three months later, Kyle sat at a table on the balcony of the newly opened Original Gus' in San Francisco. The restaurant had taken over the location of a previous burger joint on the fifth floor above a clothing store. From the balcony seats Kyle could see several blocks in each direction. The crisp late morning air pushed back and forth against the scent of freshly grilled burgers coming out of the restaurant.

"So these are all from the same cow?" Kira asked from the seat across from him.

Original Gus' prided itself on exceptionally consistent taste regardless of location. To this end all of their burger meat was made from clones of the same cow, the original Gus. Religious scholars and philosophers continued to debate whether or not this meant that Gus was constantly being reborn only to die over and over or if each clone contained its own unique variant of Gus's soul. Regardless of the metaphysics of the matter, the result was a delicious burger patty that tasted just as delicious as the previous one every time.

"No, just clones of the same cow." Kyle looked out over the balcony with a pair of binoculars.

"So, it is the same cow then?"

"No, different individual cows. Just very identical ones."

Kira shrugged and punched in her order on the tablet. She then handed it to Gretchen, Kyle's new trainee who was sitting next to him. The trainee looked over the menu intensely. The enhanced muscles in her arms rippled at the thought of cheeseburgers.

"So things must be going well with Qosi. She's already got you training people?"

"Yeah, she lost a bunch of people right before I got hired. Apparently they were all good at being sneaky, but not so good at escaping once they were caught. Lucky for her, escaping capture is something of a specialty of mine."

"You look like you still have all your limbs from the last time we met." Kira studied his arms.

"Yeah, Nadima's still got me on a probationary period. Only spare parts she deems necessary and no pills unless she says so." Kyle leaned back in his chair as their drinks arrived. "She says she'll get me some of those chemical sensors for my fingers soon though, those should be neat."

"I'm glad it's working out. Sounds like a good gig." Kira sipped her red margarita and turned towards Gretchen. "How do you like things so far Gretchen?"

"Good." Gretchen replied nervously as she pushed her long black hair out of her face. She dipped a chemical sensor equipped finger into her blue margarita and then took a sip of it. She looked over to Kyle and he nodded back to her. "Nadima is a badass boss and I really like the perks. Tasting things with my fingers took some getting used to, but now it's hard to eat anything without poking it first." She ran her fingers up and down her enhanced bicep. "These pills keep making me hungry though."

"That never goes away. Craving cheeseburgers is what helped me get to the gym this morning." Kyle grabbed his green margarita. He scanned the crowds below him with his binoculars and then froze as he zoomed in. Kyle smiled and put his binoculars down. He looked up at the sky. It was a sunny, cloudless day. A perfect day for a new lesson. "Gretchen, do you see that man in the copper colored business suit sitting at the left side table in front of the Sundeer?" Kyle handed her his binoculars.

Gretchen looked over the balcony and saw the man Kyle was referring to.

"Yeah, I see him. Want me to go down there and put my fist through his head while you two watch?" Gretchen asked.

"I like where your head is at, but no, not today." Kyle said. "Today we are working on taking out a target without making it look like a hit."

Kyle handed his phone to Gretchen.

"Why did you order a bowling ball for drone delivery to here?" Gretchen asked.

"A bowling ball? Nice choice." Kira remarked as she sipped on her margarita.

"Turn on the location tracker for the drone." Kyle

replied.

Gretchen turned on the location tracker and an arrow appeared showing, the flight path of the drone as it homed in on the phone. Kyle pointed up to the airspace above the man in the copper suit. A drone was just barely visible above the buildings and coming closer.

"Come here. I'll show you what I'm talking about." Kyle got out of his chair and went to the edge of the balcony. Gretchen followed him and brought the phone with her. The drone altered its course to get back in line to the phone.

"It moved." Gretchen said.

"Exactly, now see who's in line with it?" Kyle turned towards Kira and she gave him a thumbs up in approval.

"That guy in the copper suit!" Gretchen said with an excited hop. "But how are you going to get it to drop the bowling ball from here?"

"That's what these are for." Kyle tapped on the binoculars.

"So those aren't just to make you look like a stupid tourist?"

"No, in addition to doing that I have a gun with a silencer printed into the middle of them here. Watch this." Kyle said with confident grin.

He held up the binoculars and looked up at the drone. Through them he could see the locks on the side of the cargo box holding the bowling ball. Kyle looked back down at the target and pushed Gretchen a foot to the right. He verified that the drone was in line and turned on the rangefinder in his binoculars.

The drone closed to the correct distance and Kyle fired, blowing the lock off the container holding the bowling ball. A brand new crystal clear bowling ball with a black rose in the center of it fell out of the drone's cargo box. The bowling ball crashed onto the skull of the man in the copper suit, driving his head down through his shoulders and out his own ass. Blood burst out and splattered onto everyone sitting near the man.

Kyle put the binoculars down. His phone screen was now flashing 'Package Lost in Transit.' The people covered in blood screamed as they grabbed their cups of coffee and fled.

Gretchen's mouth hung open in astonishment. "That was amazing!"

"See, when you do things right, nobody will even know you did anything. That's why you always have to document your kills properly, otherwise you'll never get credit for the creative ones." Kyle flicked on his Hitboard account and confirmed the kill.

#bowlingwithbutthead

Kira high fived them both as they sat back down at the table.

"You get the next hit, ok?" Kyle asked Gretchen.

"You got it." Gretchen's normally tanned face flushed red with excitement. She could barely sit still in her seat.

"Now *there* is a woman who picked the right profession for herself." Kira tapped her glass to Gretchen's.

"Looks like you folks could use some burgers." A server

said as he laid their food down on the table.

"Damn right." Kyle replied. "I could kill for a cheeseburger."

ABOUT THE AUTHOR

Tom Reeve grew up in San Diego, CA. He holds a BS from UC Berkeley and a MS from the University of Michigan, both for Mechanical Engineering. He has worked primarily in the medical device industry since 2007 because it is challenging, weird and often very gross.

He currently lives in San Francisco, CA with an ever rotating cast of roommates. When he isn't busy working or writing Tom spends his time running marathons, going to random concerts, playing video games and watching cheesy movies.

You can find more updates on Tom's latest projects at www.booksbytomreeve.com

To keep up to date on upcoming books from Tom, please sign up on the mailing list here: http://eepurl.com/csXM9z

Thanks for reading!